THE WESTERN RAIDER:
SILVER TRENT RIDES ALONE
AND OTHER STORIES

SILVER TRENT RIDES ALONE
AND OTHER STORIES

By Stone Cody

STEEGER BOOKS • 2021

BLOOD ON THE YUCCA

MOONRISE PUT a yellow light over this stretch of the malpais—like a queer and malevolent forerunner of dawn. The rocks rose in twisted and tortured shapes, their shadows showing a hell's blackness against the dying dark of the night.

The moon itself looked contorted. It was past the quarter and looked like a twisted, phosphorescent fungus glowing in a black and stagnant pool.

The light showed the yellowness that had come into Trent's gray eyes—that yellow light which came into them by day and now, eerily, by moonlight, like that of a mountain cat on the prowl.

He himself was occupied only with the secret boil of his own emotions which he fought down before he answered the grim-faced man at his side.

"I've told you before—the man's my friend. Maybe you've got reason to suspect him. Maybe I have. But I've got no proof." He tried to keep his voice cool and even, but a roughness crept into it. "Since when have you heard of me turnin' against a pardner on the basis of some cantina talky-talk?" Despite himself, his voice rose a little on that, hit the quiet air with a strained explosiveness that betrayed the taut nerves inside him.

Jim Cane shrugged, and Trent could sense his over-shoulder

glance at the others which said: "Huh! He's on one of his mule-headed slants. Nothin' more to do about it."

Behind Trent, the other two kept silent. Magpie Myers was too old and wise to have braced Trent on this subject, but he had quietly given way at stocky, red-headed Jim Clane's nod, so

A withering blast of fire broke
out behind Trent's men....

as to allow Jim to ride up beside Silver Trent and say what they
all had in mind. He had dropped back and ridden, with the old
wisdom of his smile under his drooping white mustache, beside
big Lars Johannsen.

Lars said nothing also, because to his placid mind it didn't
matter if Steve Donahue was a traitor or not. If Steve was a

3

traitor, then they might be riding into a gun-trap, and that didn't seem anything much to Lars, who had ridden into other gun-traps.

Lars had a definite contempt for bullets. Although he had been shot to doll-rags more than once, and once had been so dose to death that the Grim Reaper must have subsequently felt like a Scandinavian, still Lars was convinced that bullets couldn't hurt him. So he didn't care whether Steve Donahue was a traitor or not

Trent himself stared moodily back into the magnificent eye of the moon. He had himself back from saying to Clane and the others that he would like to go on without them—that he didn't want them to take the risk that was inherent in his stubborn trust of Steve Donahue. But to offer them an out on it would be to insult them. He knew that they would stick with him, whether he insulted them or not, whether they knew the was mistaken or not. It was the penalty, the almost intolerable responsibility, of leading men who were utterly loyal. Whatever happened was your fault And yet whatever happened through your leadership, there was no way to spare the others, because they flatly refused to be spared.

He shook himself a little, increasing the pace, impatient to get to this rendezvous, which, according to Jim Clane, might easily be fatal.

The moon lifted high, but now it was losing its hot sullen brilliance. As it drifted its tortured way upward it paled, for the light of dawn began to spread vaguely, almost imperceptibly over the badlands. And with it came a little breeze, sighing past the twisted and grotesque shapes of the rocks.

With the wind came an odor—a scent almost too faint to be distinguished—of leather and the cooling smell of sweated horse.

Trent jerked his mount into a rearing halt. "Back!" he snapped to the others.

The slug whickered just in front of him and twanged off the rock face at his side. The echoing report of the shot followed a split second behind.

The riders wheeled, plunging toward their backtrail as a hammering chorus of shots broke out ahead. But they had hardly progressed two jumps before a withering blast of fire broke out from the rear.

Silver heard lead go home into flesh twice, with the wet, unmistakable sound of a solid hit, and there was the indrawn grunt that goes with the sound. He cursed under his breath savagely.

Over there a space showed between distorted rock. "Left! Follow me!" he snapped.

IN THE gray dawn light, the place looked familiar, and a moment later he knew that it was. Ahead was the entrance to a short ravine, the opening guarded by a solitary rock that jutted upward like the shape of a giant frozen yucca blossom. His hand went to the two bags that hung one on each side of his saddle horn—a small one and a larger, both so packed with greenbacks that the jingle of silver in them was muted even in that sudden

5

jerking movement. Deftly, he tossed them in one swift movement to arc upward into the cup of the yucca-shaped stone.

They sped true and fell almost soundlessly as his horse hammered past into the ravine. So quick and unobtrusive was the movement that it was doubtful if the others, following behind, had noted it. Certainly, the enemy could not have.

The ravine he followed was no more than a hundred-foot runnel between rock. Then it broke into the open, while another ravine jutted out at the right.

Instant gunfire met them as they came out of the ravine. Behind Silver, a horse went down with a sudden slam. He turned to see Magpie panned under the animal. In the dim light the old, wrinkled ace looked colorless and agonized.

Silver swung out of the saddle. Nearby was a kind of natural fort—a circle of locks standing up slabsided. His racing mind took in their possibilities as he jumped toward Magpie.

Lars Johanssen was there at the same time.

"I lift the hoss, Silver," he grunted. "You drag Magpie out."

He bent and got his huge hands under the fallen animal and lifted. Trent took hold of Magpie gently and got ready to pull him out when the weight of the horse was off him.

Lars Johannsen's great heaving muscles stood out bunched and straining. The veins leaped out on his forehead and sweat spurted from his face. Trent had never seen him try so hard or be so slow in his lift.

Then the horse's body came slowly up and he pulled Magpie free. It took only a moment to find out that the oldster's leg was broken above the knee.

BLOOD ON THE YUCCA

Silver stood up, lips compressed. And then he saw why Lars had sweated and heaved so. Lars had been hit twice—once high in the chest and again in the belly. He was breathing in great gasps, and for an instant, as Silver looked, his knees buckled a little. Presently he straightened.

"Get in the saddle, Lars," Silver said quietly.

As he spoke, lead nipped at his sleeve and snarled about his head. The attackers from the rear had come up and reached the entrance to the short ravine.

Silver dragged his guns and slammed four shots echoing down that runnel. One of the running figures went down. Another checked, staggering. The others dived for cover.

But the light was growing and the hail of lead from in front continued, was growing. Only that circle of up-ended rocks gave them partial protection, and the random storm of fire would settle soon into deadly shooting, for the light was growing every moment.

Lars was moving slowly, heavily toward his horse. Silver jumped for Magpie, whipped his belt loose, ripped down four blanches of stunted mesquite and put a splint on his leg. He picked Magpie up and set him in the saddle. Lars had gotten on his horse by now. He sat with his head drooping a little, his breath deep and harsh and uneven.

Silver took two paces to where Jim knelt behind one of the stones. "Get in the saddle, Jim," he said swiftly. "Take the ravine that branches off there. Take it at a walk, so they'll think somebody's just leadin' the horses to cover. Magpie an' Lars are both hurt bad. They're on your head."

7

Jim looked at him grimly. "An' you?" be growled.

"I stay here," Silver said quickly. "I'll buy you the time you need."

"They'll get you."

"They won't. I'll give up as soon as you're well away. This ravine leads out to the stretch of the cactus flats and over to the low rimrock wall. Half a mile beyond the yellow caves is that crack in the rock that goes back into the box canyon we was in once. There's food cached there, an' nobody'll ever find you. Stick there until Lars and Magpie are all right to ride again!"

Jim shot carefully once, and a man who had carelessly showed a head, dropped face downward.

"You do it," he said, tight-lipped and stubborn. "You know the way better than me."

Silver slammed a shot down the short arroyo and then snapped at Clane. "Do as I say, an' do it quick! Since when did you start givin' orders around here? Full daylight will be here quick. Move!"

Temper feared for an instant in Clane's eyes. "Damn you, Silver!" he said bitterly. But he got up and darted back to his horse.

IN THE growing light, Silver could see that the circle of rocks had a solid base that rose maybe two feet from the ground. It must have been one solid rock once, and parts of it had worn down in the freak conformation of the badlands, to form something like a semicircular fence of huge pickets set in a concrete foundation.

He shot from behind one rock, with his right-hand gun and

jumped a pace to the left, firing from the left side of the same rock with his other gun. Then he rolled instantly to the next rock and shot again.

Behind him he could hear the horses walking down the ravine, the slow sound of their going drowned in the hammer of gun-fire.

He had a momentary breath of relief. He had been afraid Jim would prove stubborn. But he knew now that Jim would keep on. He had two lives in his hands now, and once having undertaken the task he would not give it up, not even for the pleasure of coming back here—and getting himself killed.

Silver crawled to the next rock and shot again. By keeping moving he could give the impression that all four of them were still here and still shooting. It might gain Jim the time he needed to get clear. After that, of course, it would be full light, and the trick wouldn't work any more. Then this crowd outside would move in on him—whoever they were.

He didn't have any real thought of giving up. Likely it would mean hanging if he did. But anyway, he wouldn't have the chance. They'd get him, no doubt, even before he had been able to give the others the full time they needed.

Something slapped his ribs violently and he could feel the bone crack. A second bullet slammed the rock at his side, and a jagged splinter buried itself in his cheek. The shock of the first slug knocked him sideways and showed him the man who had fired. It was one of the gunmen in the short arroyo. He had climbed the ravine wall and was shooting down on him.

9

Silver killed him, but he knew then that his time was short, for others would try this trick, and they would not be so careless.

Then he forgot about that, because he was very busy, crawling, jumping, rolling from rock to rock, trying to shoot fast and accurately. His big muscled body felt suddenly tired. Blood kept running down his side and his face and from somewhere on his shoulder, and the full blast of the rising sun was washing the whirling moon out of existence. Had he been able to…?

The full white noonday blast of seven suns exploded against his skull, flared out into screaming starlet streamers and then detonated in a savage black cloud….

CHAPTER 2
ORDEAL OF THE CHAINS

THE SEVEN suns had merged into one sun with the strength of seven. The weight of it beat down between his shoulder blades like the impact of molten lead. It was on his head, too, hammering at it, sending steady shocks of pain through it, as though someone were wielding a sledge, "Hu-unh!—Hu-unh—Hu-unh!"

He seemed to be crouched on his knees with his forehead resting on a slab in hell. Slowly, painfully, he tried to move and found that his arms were stuck out behind, held by what appeared shackles of fire.

He fought to get his forehead up, lifted himself by pulling at his damped wrists. Pain lanced through his side.

He was on his knees, hunkered now against his heels, looking out across a courtyard full open to the glare of the sun. Figures moved about it slowly, or hunched in the thin shadow of a high wall.

Somebody said, *"Mira!* He's awake."

A buzz of comment sounded, and above it a harsh voice, still in Spanish, "Big gringo, you'll wish you could go to sleep again soon."

Raucous, mocking laughter broke out at that. "Look at him. He sits like a sick chicken."

Trent's aching eyes took in the scene before him and slowly its significance seeped through. He was in a Mexican jailyard. In front of him, on three sides of the enclosure were cells, their barred doors open now, except for one which had only a small grilled window high on the door.

He himself, he saw, was shackled to a wall, the rusty manacles on his wrists attached to chains that stapled into the adobe of the wall. The chains had given him just play enough to kneel, forehead down, with his arms stuck out behind him, when he had been chained there, unconscious.

Now, his comparatively upright posture took the strain off his wrists, but there was not yet any returning life in them—none of the raw pain that would follow when the circulation came back.

Another wall rose back of the cells, and on this a ragged figure with a rifle was perched.

"Hace despierto," he called. Then returned his gaze to the court and spat indifferently at the roof of the nearest cell.

Silver understood that it had been officially announced that he had waked up. Vaguely, he wondered why they had expected him ever to awaken. His face felt suffused, the blood congested and his head was swathed in a red blanket of heat which must be something like sunstroke. If he were actually awake, it didn't seem likely that he would be awake long.

Still, he reflected with grim irony, he ought to have service soon. No doubt the hotel staff would come running, to bathe him and feed him and offer whatever luxuries were available. Including breaking on the wheel.

He awaited their arrival without interest. Nothing could be much worse than what he felt now.

The arrival consisted in the entrance of a short, fat individual in a gaudy, if shabby, uniform, accompanied by what appeared to be a semi-military staff. At least, those with him were also in some land of uniform. Silver was particularly impressed with one lean gentleman in a blue coat with tarnished dress epaulettes and a pair of ragged cotton about which hung about his bony knees like a frayed shade about a lamp. His calves and feet were bare, but an oversized cavalry sword beat about his ankles as he walked.

The fat man looked at Silver and said, "Hah!"

"Hah!" Silver returned mildly.

The fat man looked momentarily disconcerted, but then his brows drew down in a portentous frown.

"You dare to be insolent, gringo dog?" he squeaked.

He lifted a booted foot and kicked Silver in the face. The toe of the thin-soled boot landed against Trent's cheekbone and the fat man winced involuntarily as his toes gave under the impact.

He set the foot down gingerly and said, *"Pero de bandido!*

When you speak to *El Coronel Salvador Santiago Baupez, Commandante de Leche Buena,* speak with respect—*comprend?*"

Silver deduced that he had, somehow, to deal with the military governor of Leche Buena. He had heard that a new man had been sent into this district-some politico from Mexico City—but until now he had never met him.

He didn't get all of it yet, so he kept silent.

"Where is the money you stole, bandit?" the commandante demanded fiercely. "Do not attempt to lie to me. I know that you had it and that you gave it to one of your *compadres* to carry. Where is it now?"

Silver looked at him and ease flowed over his soul. He knew his danger now, but it was a warm relief, for he knew then, also, that Jim and the others had gotten away clean. Otherwise, this fat fool would not have phrased his question the way he did.

Silver grinned at him wickedly. *"Gordo,"* he said, and he let the amused insolence go full in his voice. "What money are you talking about? It must be the gold you dream of in your swollen, glutted guts."

The commandante looked stunned for a long instant. Evidently it was inconceivable to him that a man in Silver's position would dare such impudence. And there was a long, audible catching of breath among his riff-raff followers.

Then the fat man squalled, "You'll pay for this, *insolente.* You'll end by crawling to me to beg me to listen to where the money is."

But in his rage, he had come too close. Silver kicked out and caught him in the lower belly. The fat man doubled over with an anguished cry. At Silver's side a man jumped, cursing, and swung something that put midnight into this glare of noon....

WHEN TRENT came to again, he was cramped in a cell which was blacker than the heart of Hell and stunk of a generation of prisoners who had been denied the hygienic facilities of ordinary men.

The wound in his ribs ached agonizingly and the wound on his head, reopened by his recent blow, shed drops of red pain that flowed through his hair and down his neck. His cheek ached and all the muscles of his body were in savage foment.

He lay still, remembering. The fat man had a weak, vainglorious chin. He looked like a swollen toad with brown cruel eyes. But he was not back of all this. He was somebody's instrument. It was unlikely that he had the brain to plot the shrewd, complete trap into which Silver had ridden. And besides that, he couldn't have known about the money. Somebody—the man behind him—must have known about that.

The thought of Steve Donohue came into Silver's mind, and for a moment, red hate hazed his brain Steve Donohue knew about the money. That smaller sack of the two which Silver had thrown up into yucca stone had been Steve's cut—two thousand dollars, out of ten.

Eight thousand dollars! Would a man plot murder for that? A hundred thousand murders had been plotted for a tenth of that, and less!

But Steve... Silver shook his head unbelievingly. Steve hadn't seemed like that And what evidence had he? Some cantina gossip and—an ambush. Word might have been flashed ahead of the way they would probably ride. Or....

But whatever he thought of seemed unlikely. How would anyone but Steve know which way they would ride?

Yet Steve Donohue had been his friend....

He groaned almost inaudibly in the dark, and then drifted wearily into a troubled sleep.

He woke again in bright daylight, with sunshine coming hot and bright through the bars of his cell. His throat felt half closed and his lips cracked and swollen. He wondered how long ago it had been since he had had water.

There were yells and catcalls from the cells alongside and somebody shouted, "Beans! Where are the beans without *carne?* Where are the beans without *enchilados?* Where are the beans without *gusto?*"

After a little, Silver's cell door swung open. A guard stood in the doorway with a tin plate of beans in his hands. Behind him was another guard with a rifle held ready.

The guard did not come up to Silver, who was held by an ankle iron affixed to the wall, but merely slid the plate of beans within reach and grinned evilly. "These are *segundos,*" he said. "The raw beans that other men tried to digest and could not."

Silver looked at the plate. "I think you must be wrong, my friend," he said lightly, tapping one of the beans, "for this one is surely ripe, and that other—well... something about it."

He gave an appearance of being elaborately bored, uninterested further in the dish before him.

"What about that other?" the guard asked suspiciously.

"Nothing," Silver shrugged. "Nothing at all."

"Don't try to fool me, gringo dog," the guard said angrily. "You'll be the worse for it if you do."

"Don't try to fool me," Silver said grimly. "I know that what looks like a diamond is only glass. Go on about your business. I, too, was fooled for a minute, but—"

The guard's avid eye fixed on the plate. "Diamond? Where?" he growled half suspiciously.

"Go on about your business," Silver said nervously.

The guard took a step forward, reached down for the plate.

Silver's hand shot out like a lizard's tongue, jerked him forward.

The guard in the doorway cried out and lifted his gun, but his compadre was in the line of fire.

Silver had the first guard by the throat, the pressure of his fingers forcing his mouth open. With his other hand he scooped up the plate, forced the raw mess into the guard's mouth. Then he put his hand over the guard's mouth and released his grip on the throat. The man swallowed convulsively, swallowed again, gasped, as Silver forced the stuff down his throat.

Then Silver sent him slamming backwards into the arms of the ether guard. "If you've got any left," Silver said grinning, "you might give 'em to your friend."

Madly, the guard seized his companion's gun and slammed its butt at Silver. But Silver drew back, missing the blow and the next one. The Mexican paused, breathing hard, caught now by the shut gray, deadly gaze of Silver's eyes.

16

"You-you'll pay for that," he panted. But he turned away, and as he did, his face was sick.

IT WAS an hour later that they brought Silver out. They were very careful about the mechanics of it, and this time they chained him to the wall with his face toward his manacles. And he knew then that he was going to feel the lash.

Later he heard footsteps, and the voice of the fat commandante: "You had better tell where your compadres are holed-up," the commandante said. "That way we will know where the money is, and maybe it won't go so hard with you."

Silver looked over his shoulder and cursed him and his forebears elaborately and with great detail, ending, "It is thus that you are born to be a shame among men."

The commandante screamed. And then his hate overflowed in a babbling spate of rage.

He told Silver about his ancestors, he told him about the rotten cells of his soul which would shortly sicken the vampires of hell. He told him he knew about the cattle deal for which Silver had gotten ten thousand dollars, for running mangy Mexican cattle over the river into Arizona. He snarled that he knew of Silver's other activities—namely, running wet Texas cattle into Mexico.

He howled that Silver had made a false reputation as a great leader of bandits, but that he would be broken here and now. He would be broken here, and all the prisoners who watched would be set free to spread the word of the great Hawk's craven crawling. He yelled that Silver had only one chance of escaping this vengeance of all decent men—and that was to tell where he had sent the money, where his men were hiding. And that maybe—just *maybe*—Silver might still have a chance of being killed decently if he told, but that otherwise he would be made into a shrieking Thing for all men to jeer at.

Silver slid, "Why bother about those three? I have other men who will shortly be here and who will make the sign of the cross on your fat belly with good sharp steel."

The commandante howled, his voice choked with fury and triumph. "You fool! Your men are done for—finished. They were sent word that you were in trouble, and ambushed! Those who are not dead are scattered and running for their lives."

The tone of it, the howling exultant fury behind it, convinced Silver that it was true. There are notes of the voice, intonations, which are beyond doubt, which come to Truth itself.

He felt his spine chill, his blood run cold. And for a long moment the fight went out of him. So… By trusting Steve Donohue he had not only sacrificed the three who were with him, but all the rest of the men he loved, his Hawks—*Los Halcones de los Sierras*—Ricardo, the intrepid; Pablo, the lean and furious friend of the Saints; Jim Lang, who had been a Ranger until the fire of his sense of Justice had driven him to the long and lonely trail, and… Then a kind of merciful blackness came into him, shutting off the thought of them.

"So you might as well tell where the others are, and the money!" the commandante yelled. "Or you'll take the three-pronged cactus! Will you tell?"

"Go with God," Silver said, his voice harsh and broken on

the old Spanish phrase, "so that He may kick you down to the Hell where you belong!"

The commandante's voice was a strangled squawk. "Give it to him."

And the lash fell.

It was called the three-pronged cactus because it had three thongs that went out in somewhat the shape of a pitchfork when the whistling air held them apart. And the thongs had sharp stones knotted at intervals.

The flesh of Silver's back shrank as the lash whistled home into his back.

It came again. And again. Raw agony screamed from his straining back. He jerked, maddened at the chains that held him to the wall, but the sole result was to bring blood spurting from his wrists. And again the barbed lash fell, and again.

So they had gotten his men. Somebody would pay dear for that. Maybe it was Steve Donohue; maybe not. But somebody. And now he must live, must endure this, for he had important work to do….

He could tell about the money and still save his men. But if he told about the money he might never know whether Steve Donohue… But already he thought of a plan….

The strength went out of his knees, out of his belly.

"Tell!" It was the voice of the commandante shrieking faintly in his ears. "Tell, and maybe you will live!"

And then the leather and stone bit flesh again.

He thought: *They want the money bad, but what they want most*

19

of all is to break Silver Trent. If they can break me like this, publicly, no man will ever follow me again.

The whistling impact came again, raised agony in his back, sent the vicious shock clear to his knees.

Frantically, he jerked at his bonds. They gave a little on the right hand. Or did they? No. The iron held firm in the adobe.

CHAPTER 3
OVER THE WALL TO HELL

THE WORLD swayed and whirled about him. For a moment in its periphery, he saw figures, faces, prisoners crouched close to the wall, staring, their facts tense and horrified. But one laughed, jeered in an ecstasy of cruel enjoyment. He recognized the man who had guffawed loudest at him the day before. A thick-built, powerful, pockmarked man with cruel, reptilian eyes.

The lash fell again.

Somewhere near him a voice groaned, gasping, in utter agony. He wondered who it was, and then realized that it was himself.

Faintly, vaguely, as in a dim nightmare a squeaking, sickish toad voice came to him, *"Dios!* Men die of forty, and he has taken fifty. Better let him—"

The voice blacked out as the blows fell once more. And then there was no more....

It would be three days before they could profitably whip him again.

But on the second day he was allowed to crawl out among the prisoners.

He found that they gathered themselves into two groups. Those who were profoundly impressed by the punishment he had taken, and those whose gringo hatred was still to the fore, glad and triumphant because the man who had been great in the countryside was now nothing, as they were nothing; as they had always been nothing.

He had seen the hatred in their eyes that first day. Now he saw it still. It hit him hard. It was true—he tried to remember it—that this was the scum of the people, the criminals, the riff-raff, the ne'er-do-wells.

Yet this still was the people he had tried to help. No man north or south of the Border had ever been able to say that Silver Trent or any single one of his Hawks had robbed a poor man. In very fact he had taken from the rich to give to the poor, as a great man had done before him. And everywhere he had gone, the poor people had helped him, had seemed—damned uncomfortably for him—to worship him.

And now that he was down, this mob had turned against him.

It was bitter. But also, maybe there was right in it.

He had been treated like a god, and he was only a man. It was true that he was big, with the sloping shoulders of natural power more violent than any he had ever encountered—except the enormous power of Lars Johanssen's outsized muscles. And he was fast. A shade faster in a fight or with a gun than anybody he had met. Yet he was only a man. Square faced, tough featured, with a single white lock of hair which had given him his nick-name—Silver. But ordinary enough.

The bad luck was that he had had too good luck. He had succeeded, by some sense and much luck, in being the most spectacularly successful bandit in Mexico. And so men had romanticized him. Had called him the Hawk. Had called his men The Hawks of the Mountains—*Los Halvones de las Sierras.* And his men had accepted that and made it into their battle cry—*"A nosotros, Los Halcones*—to us, the Hawks—Hell's Hawks for Trent!"

It had been a rallying cry that had waked the echoes of the high hills and the low, that had lifted to the red skies of dawn and sunset on the plains—a cry for which plain men had thanked God, and that crooks had cursed.

But his luck had endured too long....

Ah, well-too late for all that! He was here now, and no doubt the thing was ended. His men were scattered and broken. Those who might guess where he was were wounded, holing up by his own orders, and he himself was caught by men who feared him just enough not to give him the smallest chance.

It wax no doubt, the finish. But one thing he would not do—he could not give in. Not even enough to tell them where the money was. And God knew that wasn't important, except as to how it might affect Steve Donohue, whom he would never see again, anyway.

This battered hulk, crawling about with the flies swarming and buzzing, this was Silver Trent, who had the misfortune to be tough enough to suffer a little longer than he should have, but who couldn't last long now....

It was morning again, with his face to the wall, and the fat commandante, Baupez, again behind him.

This time they had a flail of narrow chains, instead of the rope and rock. And there was a new look of triumph in Baupez' eye.

"A dog should be whipped by dogs," Baupez said pontifically. "Let a prisoner whip him."

Very nice, Silver thought. This is in the scheme to break me. I am to be whipped by a low-caste man. So therefore all the people will know, even though I don't break, that I have been humiliated beyond shame.

They were choosing a man to wield the flail. Silver saw that he was decent-enough looking; a man who had tried to speak to him and who had even saved him a little of his own water, for Silver's lips were cracked with thirst and fever. He might have been, Silver reflected, the man who would—under different circumstances—ridden with the famous Hawks.

This man's name was Avila, Silver remembered, and his face was pale, reluctant Yet if he did not obey, he himself would be beaten.

"Go ahead, friend," Silver said, out of the corner of his mouth. "I won't hold it against you."

The man looked at him, his cheeks and mouth going gray-white under his brown skin.

He took the flail and balanced it in a trembling hand. He raised it. Then he dropped his arm again and swung to face the guards and the commandante.

23

"I won't do it," he said in a shaking voice. "Do whatever you want to me, but I won't do this to Silver Trent."

THEY CURSED him, struck him down, but there was no moving that frightened man. Silver tried to tell him again to go ahead, but the man was not listening. His head was bowed with the stubbornness of a bull awaiting the kill.

"I'll do it! Let me!" It was the squat, powerful, pockmarked man who spoke—the man who had laughed and jeered.

There was an almost whining eagerness in his voice.

Baupez snapped, "Give him the flail!" A guard kicked Avila in the belly and took the chains from him.

The pockmarked man seized them eagerly. Silver turned to face the wall, setting his legs squarely and tensing the big tough muscles of his wrists. His back muscles strained, his arms bulged.

The pockmarked man swung the flail, putting the force of his body into it. It whistled through the air and the thin steel links bit into Silver's flesh.

The straining power of his body stiffened, heaved backward in a vein-bursting effort. The staple that held the hand on his right gave a little in crumbling adobe, came loose in a little burst of greyish powder.

Silver turned and swung the heavy chain, with the thick staple whirling at the end of it.

The pockmarked man's eyes bulged. He gave a gasping cry, chopped the flail and tried to dodge. Then the swinging chain caught him just above the ear.

The savage links bit into flesh and bone, came close to taking off the top of his head. The man was dead before his squat body hit the ground.

The swing about brought a new vista into Silver's gaze. It showed him the doorway which led into the court from the jail's office. And in the shadows there was a figure he knew—Avila Toledano!

The big, bull-necked Mexican was lurking there in the shadows behind the doorway. But he wasn't any longer jovial, hearty. He was staring at Silver with his mouth twisted and savage hostility in his eyes.

Silver felt dazed. For this was the same man who had been his patron in recent cattle raids. It had been him with whom Steve Donohue had been in contact. Avila Toledano had bought the wet cattle which Silver and his men brought in from Texas. Avila Toledano had given them their tips so that they would know where cattle were gathered, and could be run off easily here in Mexico.

Avila Toledano had professed himself the enemy of crooked and ruthless cattlemen on both sides of the Border and therefore had appeared to be delighted to be Silver's accomplice in taking toll of them. Yet Avila Toledano was here, in the background—as Baupez' guest!

Silver's left arm jerked and strained.... And as though the crumbling adobe had been waiting only for this surge of anger, the staple came free.

The fat commandante squawked like a terrified hen and ran spraddled legged toward the door where Toledano stood. He clawed the bars open. One of the guards followed him, forgetting the gun in his hand. The other gave back, yellow-faced, grabbing frantically for the sixgun at his belt, and missing it in his panic.

Silver jumped for him, jerked the six-gun free and then leaped back. The guard on the wall had galvanized into action. He ran, his rifle at the ready, to where he could get a shot at Silver.

Unluckily for him, he got too close. Silver swung his left-hand chain. It hurtled upward, hit the guard's rifle, looped around it. Silver jerked, and the rifle came clattering down into the court.

From the doorway to the office a gun hammered, its blast smashing at Silver's ears in the hot morning air.

He tipped up the sixgun he had taken from the guard and shot back. Somebody yelled in panic, and the passageway cleared like magic.

On the wall, the guard had frozen, fear in his eyes, but now he ran back and jumped, chancing the twenty-foot drop to the ground below.

Silver whirled, caught sight of the pale, excited face of Lazaro, the man who had refused to whip him. He thrust the rifle into the man's hands.

"Up!" he snapped, "I'll toss you up."

He caught him and threw him to the roof of the cells. "Now! Catch the chain," he commanded.

He was about to throw his left arm chain upward when a hand clutched his arm.

"Let me go, too, señor!"

IT WAS the scrawny skeleton of a man whose whipcord

muscles seemed to be attached to his bones without flesh or skin, like an anatomical drawing.

Before Silver could speak, another prisoner jumped forward. "On my shoulders, señor," he cried, "and you afterwards, old one!"

He stood crouching, his heavy bade bent, and he was big for a Mexican. Silver caught the corded skeleton and swung him to the big man's back. An instant later the lean arms had caught the roof and were pulling upward.

Silver's foot touched the big back before him, seemingly lightly, yet the impact of his weight nearly knocked the man from his feet. Then Silver was on the roof.

He swung his chain down. "Grab it, and hang on!" he snapped.

He had a glimpse of blazing eyes below him and then he heaved as the man caught hold. And one great heave did it.

The other prisoners were still transfixed, staring in the yard. Their attitudes and tension, the fear and astonishment that still looked from their eyes, gave Silver a gauge of how short the time had been.

With the others, Silver jumped then for the wall. But below, a soldier in a nondescript uniform cried out. Silver shot him in the thigh and jumped down again.

Guards began to boil out of the jail building. Half a dozen soldiers in a nearby courtyard yelped, grabbing up arms and came running.

Silver slammed a shot right and left. The skeletal man jumped for the soldier who had been shot in the thigh and grabbed his gun. Lazaro fired blindly into the soldiers in the courtyard.

27

Under the noise of the gunshots and the running feet a voice sounded, trembling, fat-sounding even in its panic. *"Mi caballo! Pronto, hombre!"*

It came, faint but extraordinarily clear in the hot air. Silver called, "This way!" And jumped for the alley that led toward the side entrance of the jail. Even as he moved there came horses at the dead gallop.

He was in time to see them racing up the street—the commandante, Toledano and two others. He slung a fast shot at them, but they were almost out of range and the slug missed. Then they whirled around a corner and were gone.

Silver smiled grimly and walked back to where the guards had taken cover in the prison adobe. "Your bosses have left on the run," he called in Spanish. "Come out. If you come out, you'll be safe. If you don't, we'll come in after you."

They came out. And the soldiers yielded to the same treatment.

Silver saw that there was a sudden, eagerly pressing crowd around him. That is, those behind pressed forward, but those in front fought to hold back, their eyes respectful and pleading. Somebody shouted: *"Viva el Halcon."* And the crowd took it up with a roar.

Silver held up his hand. "Hombres!" he called out, "give back. Let us have order. You have seen your fine commandante run as the jackrabbit runs."

He paused, eyeing them sardonically, but no wound had touched the gray iron of his eyes.

"You were not in a hurry to help me before, were you?" he

asked gently. "But now you're on my side—add this is my town. Why wasn't it like that before? You knew me well—at least by reputation. You knew I was the friend of the poor and oppressed. But you did not come to cheer me then, when there were a few guns and a little authority against you. Now that I have taken these few guns and chased out this little fat authority, you have come to cheer me. Are you men or coyotes? I do not think that I am very proud of you, citizens."

A sudden, wholly abashed silence followed his words.

HE TURNED to the others, those who had escaped with him, the bitter chill still in his eyes. "And you?" he murmured. "You are free now. I take it that was what you wanted. But tell me, I'm curious. Since you were not sentenced to death, why did you take such a long chance? Didn't you have time to think that the chances were ten to one that I would be killed the moment I went over the wall? Why did you come?"

The big man looked uneasy, and Lazaro's cheeks showed pale as though he bad been slapped. But the oldster spoke up and his eyes flared.

"We saw the jackals run when the lion was loose," he said. "And for those whose liver is not pale, it is better to die with the lion than feed with the jackal."

Silver's hard gaze warmed a little. "Spoken like a man, old one," he said.

The corded skeleton bowed a little over his hand, *"Gracias, señor—mil gracias. Y voy a Usted con Dios."*

But the big man was not satisfied. He spoke eagerly to Silver. "Señor, I would ride with you. Let me be one of you—a Hawk."

29

The thought crossed Silver's mind that if what he had heard was true, there were few Hawks left. It might be a good time to start recruiting. But what he said, hard-eyed, was: "What makes you think you are fit to be a Hawk, hombre?"

The man hesitated, then blustered a little. "Señor, I am afraid of no man."

The oldster spat. "Because you are big," he snapped disgustedly. "And too big in the head. *No se que los Halcones son muchos hombres?* Do you not know that the Hawks are much men?"

"To be a Hawk requires more than to be not afraid of a man whom you can whip," Silver said. "Not to be afraid is a fool's virtue. It would be easier, perhaps, for Lazaro here to be a Hawk, for he knows fear, but he can conquer it. And to do that is to be *mucho hombre.*"

"Still, more than that is required to be a Hawk," Silver said to him. "Would you take a message for me, amigo?"

"Si, señor!" Lazaro's eyes blazed.

Silver took him aside. "I want you to find a man named Steve Donohue. To find him may be dangerous. I think he would be at Señor Toledano's hacienda; maybe free—maybe a prisoner. But let him think I am in jail—you do not know where. Tell him—remember this well!—that he will find his drink in the dew of the yucca. Understood?"

Lazaro drew a deep breath and repeated the message. "Go on then," Silver said softly. "But do not let anyone else know of this. And above all do not repeat the message to anyone but Steve Donohue."

Two minutes later Silver was in the saddle of a borrowed horse and on his way to find Jim and Lars and Magpie.

Toledano and the commandante had not ridden far, he reflected frowning. They'd round up reinforcements. They would take the town back. Moreover, Silver himself couldn't be very popular there now, with the townsmen he had virtually insulted.

The long solid line of his mouth set bitterly as he ran and walked his borrowed mount up into the hills. The hills rose to a broken ridge, dipped, and became suddenly, like black magic, the badlands.

After a long while, he came to the yucca stone. He remembered how he and Steve Donohue had sat beneath that, one sunblasted noon, hugging its queer shadow. It lifted tall, four times the height of a man, its stem like that of a yucca, its spreading top like the yucca lily.

CHAPTER 4
ARMY OF THE DAMNED

T HEY HAD talked about it, lying lazy in the thin blue shadow, while the blasting light ran its course in the sky and the land paled and glittered angrily beneath it.

They had talked of that and other things; of men and death and laughter, and the uplifted arms of dancing girls that were like disease coarsened yuccas, and of the dark eyes of señoritas… darkness of the star-sown night.

Yes, Steve would understand his message that his share of the loot was in the dew of the yucca. And he would come if he was free to come; and if he was an honest man he would take his share and leave the rest....

The trail led finally at dusk to the slab of rock that made a slit door into the canyon where the others must be.

"Pull up, hombre! And don't move!"

Silver said quietly, "Hullo, Jim."

Lars, he found, was very weak, but not nearly as dead as he might to have been. And Magpie was a little green at the corners of the mouth, but chipper enough in his splints.

Silver ate and slept, not knowing until he was relaxed, just how all in he was.

The smell of sourdough biscuits and bacon drifted into his nostrils at dawn, and he sat up, abruptly ravenous.

He ate half a dozen eggs, the last of the cache. Silver wolfed them, not knowing they were the last.

Then he put his hand on Magpie's shoulder and grinned at Lars, fighting down the guilt inside him, and said: "I got to be ridin' amigos, but I'll be back."

Jim Clane's eyes brightened. "I'll be ridin' with you," he said.

Silver shock his head. "Magpie an' Lars—"

"Magpie can walk with the crutch I fixed for him," Jim snapped. "The's still food an' water. I'm ridin' with you."

Silver hesitated, then saw Jim's eyes and nodded. Jim was as good a man as he had, but Jim's faded sandy hair had once been red. There was a time not to cross him.

Afternoon found them at the yucca rock.

They waited there, out of sight of the rock until the next morning.

Jim was puzzled. Lazaro should have had time to get to Steve by now, and Steve to come here twice over.

Finally, he said, because of Jim's violent, brooding impatience: "Look, Jim, there's more to this than meets the eye. An' this is the way to find out what's what. Toledano is crocked—against us. I couldn't figure he could be, because—besides talkin' easy an' fair, he was makin' too good a thing out of what we was doin'. But I know now he was settin' us up for a good haul, meanin' to take the money for it an' then set himself up in the same business, but without us. He figured that if we could run cattle, he could too—an' make more profit."

"And Steve Donohue was with him on it," Jim snapped. "It'd be just dumb enough for that cluck. Imagine tryin' take things over by tryin' to jump us four—with all the rest of the gang runnin' free. Why, no matter what they did to us, they'd get a bellyful of lead."

Silver's jaw set. "I didn't want to tell Lars and Magpie," he said quietly, "because they're bad hurt. But—I've heard that Toledano had the rest of the boys jumped. They're said to be scattered and run out of the country."

Jim stiffened, eyes blazing. "Silver, you know that cain't be true!"

Silver shook his head. "I don't know. It might be true or part true, or not at all true. But this Toledano has been playin' 'em close to his belly. He fooled me plenty. An' if he's not a fool, why wouldn't he go after the rest of the gang?

"He was in a position to, because the boys knew we worked with him. My guess is that he tried it. But anyway, none of the boys know where we are. And it's not likely that we could get to them in time to do us any good. Either it's you an' me against this whole setup, or it's you an' me an' Steve. He's the answer to it. If he's crooked, well, that's one thing. If he's straight—"

"Straight!" Jim spat fiercely. "Would he have led us into an ambush if—"

"*Sh-h-h!*" Silver's urgent hiss cut him off. "Somebody's comin'."

There was the stumbling scuff of leather against rock. And then a man hove into view—or nearly a man.

HE WAS half dad, his skin red-blazing under the bite of the sun. His shirt hung from him in tatters. And he did not walk so much as balance himself on one foot and then fall forward on the other.

He came weaving and lurching toward the yucca stone—a tortured scarecrow, a kind of human travesty. He had a lariat in his hand and when he got up to the stone he tried to loop it over a projection that formed one of the leaves.

Silver put a hand on Jim's arm.

The scarecrow finally hit it right. He got the rope on. Then he fastened it below and began to climb. It was pitiful to see him try it, fail, and try again.

Silver had to know... And he had to have Jim know.

And somehow this scarecrow ghost that had been Steve Donohue got to the top, hooked his hands over the top of the yucca stone and heaved upward.

For a moment he was lost to sight in that stone cup. Then he reappeared, standing upright, hefting two sacks in his hands and looking over his shoulder at the direction from which he had come. He put the bigger sack down again and slid fumblingly down the rope with the smaller one.

Silver let his breath out softly and got up. "Hello, Steve," he said.

Steve Donohue looked at him, his eyes blazing with recognition. "Silver!" he cried. "I thought they had you in jail! I was goin' to buy enough men to get you out. *Hombre*—how the devil did you get here?"

He broke off at the sound of a shod hoof sliding on loose rock.

Silver saw a sombrero and the tossed head of a cayuse against the rocks two hundred yards ahead. Instinctively his hand ripped to his saddle gun.

But the rider had not been unprepared. The crack of a Winchester whipped across the bright air.

"Up!" Silver snapped, "up behind Jim! We got to light out of here."

Steve Donohue staggered forward, climbed up behind Jim. "But Silver," he gasped. "That's Toledano, an' God only knows how many more. A double-loaded host—"

"Get goin' toward town," Silver snarled.

As he spoke, he shot. The head of the man who had shot at him jerked a little, and then swayed forward in a slow, respectful bowing motion.

"Town?" Jim fairly yelped the question. "You tryin to git us hung?"

Silver looked at him. "Maybe you'd like to do as I say, Jim," he said dangerously. "Or you still think you know it all?"

35

Color like aged brick stained Jim's face. Silver knew that he was remembering what he had thought about Steve Donohue and realizing just how right Silver had been about Steve.

Wordlessly, Jim rode off.

Silver, down behind a rock now, smiled faintly. Just as well to get Jim's mind off this present danger. Otherwise he might have balked and stayed—which would have been fatal.

He picked out another man's head and squeezed the trigger. The head went down and stayed down.

A shoulder showed and he slapped that down as neatly as though he had been shooting ducks in a gallery.

But there were a lot of them—a good twenty, he guessed.

He had gotten into the saddle when the bullet hit him. It was like an infant's sledgehammer wielded by a giant, hitting him in the back of the shoulder.

It tapped him so lightly that the feel of it was nothing, except that it drove him forward so that his forehead slapped against the neck of his horse.

Then he was away, with his mount's hoofs hammering down a narrow steep arroyo, and nothing the matter with him except that his whole body felt sick.

Later, he dimly heard the hammer of hoofs behind him and he turned his horse into the space between an outjutting rock and pulled out his rifle.

A rider came at a swift run and Silver shot him out of the saddle. As he levered another shell into the dumber, two more came into view, and he shot the first of them. The other whirled and escaped Silver's third shot.

He heard a shout and then the fading sound of excited conference.

He turned his horse and rode on, slowly.

THIS WAS what he had meant to do—hold up the pursuit long enough to give the double loaded horse a fair chance. Once Jim and Steve got into town, they could get fresh horses and get out again. It was the only chance—unless he was willing to lead Toledano to the hideout where Lars and Magpie lay wounded.

As for himself, he could keep ahead of the pursuit as long as they were in the badlands. When he hit the flat country near town, it would be touch and go. But he'd have a start and he'd he likely to make it. A few judicious bullets over his shoulder would slow the pursuit.

This was in his mind, but what was in his body was pain and shock which wore off too slowly to let him think much. His mind, still red and hazy, was dominated only by one idea when he turned a corner of rock formation and came on Jim Clane and Steve Donohue. Steve still sat the rear of the horse, his head lolling a little in sheer exhaustion, but Jim had gotten down with a rifle.

"What are you tryin' to do to us?" he demanded fretfully. "Tryin' to get yourself killed so we can go on? I heard the shooting. I know what you're tryin'."

Silver got down from his horse. He did not know that he looked almost as much like a scarecrow as Steve Donohue. The clothes he wore came near to being an insecure loincloth. His face was gaunt and his eyes pools of outraged bell.

Those eyes held Jim suddenly paralyzed for a moment. "I've

taken a lot from you, Jim," Silver said evenly. "You're red-headed and temperish, and you're one of the best men I ever had. You can shoot like lightnin' an' you're a fast, hard man with your fists. You're the exact opposite of yellow. An' you're a pain in the neck.

"I've tried to put up with your bull-headedness the best way I could. But, by God, when this is over, if you don't take my orders like the rest do—an' each one's as good a man as you, or better—I'll shoot you deader'n Adam's tomcat!"

His right fist swung. It took Jim Clane squarely between the eyes. The little knuckle of Silver's fist broke Jim's nose as a bullet would smash a ripe tomato. The blow knocked Jim seven good feet away. He did not get up.

"Take him up!" he snapped at Steve Donohue. "Tie him behind the saddle an' ride to town with him. Pick up horses there."

Donohue looked at him and then caught his breath. "I think I will," he said softly. "Yes, I think I will." And he did.

Silver's mind was a red and furious daze and his body a special hell too tortured to handle itself. But he managed to hold them off and give himself a long start toward town.

He hammered into town and somebody yelled, "Seelver! Amigo!"

It was the ex-prisoner—the man who had proclaimed that he "wasn't afraid of anybody," because he was big.

Silver swayed in the saddle, his voice ragged. "Hombre, Toledano and his crowd are on my tail. Run!"

The big ex-prisoner paled. "Then we must fight, amigo," he

yelled. "How many has he?" He looked as though he were about to faint.

"Two dozen," Silver gasped. "What man will get me a horse?" He could hardly sit the saddle.

A chorus of voices yelled. "I will, señor."

"Un momento, señor."

"Your friends are there, *Señor Halcon*. We will get you a horse also."

"Viva los Halcones."

Silver stared at them dazedly.

"Get him then a horse," yelled the big man. "But for us, let us fight!"

"But we are a bare dozen, hombre. Against Toledano's gun-fighters, it is too little."

"Too little for El Señor Seelver?" a new voice cut in. It was Lazaro, shaking still, but blazing-eyed. *"Viva Seelver!"*

"Viva! Viva!" The high pitched shout left no doubt of the temper of these men.

But as they shouted, the racing pound of hoofs sounded at the end of the street.

"They come, señor—they come!" Lazaro yelled. "Let us fight!"

Silver looked at him and the others. "Why, yes," he said softly, "let us fight." And he got down out of the saddle.

"Ah, señor—gracias!" It was the old prisoner who seemed only muscle attached to bone. "That is all we wanted to hear!"

They had come running from all sides.

CHAPTER 5
"HELL'S HAWKS FOR TRENT!"

N OW, AS the thunder of hoofs swept down the street, they scattered, terrified, except for a small dozen. And these were armed with knives, and some with old rifles, and a few with pistols, but it was no army to face this onrush of experienced fighting men.

Silver hesitated. But even in the weakness which ran through him and made his feet and arms seem like lead, he knew that to hesitate or to run would be wholly wrong. They might lose. Indeed they were sure to lose, but the defeat itself would be a kind of victory for these poor peons who had never stood up to anyone before. And so he had to fight.

He put his rifle to his shoulder, and when the first rider came into sight he squeezed the trigger. The man lurched sideways and then looked as though he were diving out of the saddle. The three riders, following close, pulled up rearing and ducked for cover as Silver shot again.

That was only the first surprise. They would come on, feel them out, understand their weakness. For there was nothing here to defend—only a few adobe shacks.

The pound of racing hoofs from the rear sent him whirling about. Jim Clane and Steve Donohue pulled up by him.

Jim Clane's mouth was set, his eyes hostile. "You want us to run or stay?"

Silver looked at him a moment—at the red heat of his eyes

and the nose spread out over his hard-jawed face. And then he snapped, "Stay! We got a fight on."

He led them out of that street, for it was no place to be closed in on. His memory turned up the one place in town where they might make a stand, use alcalde's building. It stood in the square, a short distance from all the other buildings. Vulnerable from every side it was, but defensible from every side also. And there was the chance of a quick retreat down an alley not too far from the rear door.

But they never reached there.

It appeared that Toledano had thought of it first. He had sent men around to cut them off.

A withering volley of fire met them as they emerged into the square, driving them back. Lazaro, at Silver's side, gasped and sank down despairingly. The man who was not afraid turned and whispered, "Señor, we must run."

"So you're afraid," Silver said, with calculated scorn.

"Afraid?" The big man lifted himself proudly. "No one makes Ygnacio afraid!"

Silver grinned. "Then fight, hombre. For now is the time for it."

Time, truly. For now the attack came instantly from the rear. They were caught in a trap. The alley showed only the blank back walls of adobe buildings. Behind was gunfire, and also in front. And there was no cover.

Silver Trent didn't remember when he had led anyone into such a fix. He wondered if just a little beating and a few wounds and a shot in the shoulder had really changed him into an idiot.

He distributed his forces according to their poor armament and told them to lie close to the ground and not waste any shots. He himself took the rear side, because he guessed that the force of the attack would come there.

For a little while he was able to keep the street cleared, with one gun, hammering and deadly, after another. But then the guns had to be reloaded and during that time men filtered into the street, into doorways, into every scrap of cover.

A shot creased his scalp, and put him out of the fight for a moment. And after that, something tugged at his shoulder.

Toledano's high-pitched voice screamed from a building top, "They're wrapped! Go at them! You've got them!"

It was as though the voice had been a cue. A high-pitched Mexican voice yelled, "Seelver! Are you there?"

There was the pound of hoofs.

Silver lifted his own deep-throated yell. "This way, Pablo! We're here!"

He snapped at the others. "Back! Back now to the square!"

For that was the way Pablo was coming, with the rest of his Hawks.

"Trent! Trent! Hell's way for Trent!" a great drunken voice bellowed, which would be Doc Brimstone's. Behind him a deep-throated chorus lifted. *"A nosotros!* Hell's Hawks for Trent!"

It bellowed and echoed down the narrow streets, with a quality in it to chill a man's spine—deep-throated, wild and piercing as the trump of the Lord. It was the battle cry of the Hawks, and it was raised by enough throats so that Silver knew Toledano had not succeeded in doing much to scatter or to harm his men.

BLOOD ON THE YUCCA

"A nosotros, los Haclones," he shouted, his voice deep and almost shaking with triumphant relief.

AT THE end—which came almost with the mad charge of Silver's Halcones—they broke and ran, the Toledano men—those who could.

Of those who could not, Toledano himself was one. Silver's plunging, staggering legs carried him into a side alley and through to the street to cut Toledano off.

"You—" he started. But he broke off because the scarecrow that was Steve Donohue was there before him. He also had cut Toledano off and the Mexican *Haciendero* had turned to face Steve.

"You used me like a fool," Steve Donohue was saying savagely. "By God, you used me to make a fool out of Silver. But you didn't get away with it, did you? You thought that you could take me and torture me into saying where you could find Silver with the money. You thought you could take Silver and break him in your jail. You thought you could run cattle better than us. You crawling, slimy skunk! But you got me to face now!"

"You—I—listen, Steve," Toledano was babbling. "Steve—*Steve!*"

The three shots of Steve Donohue's sixgun sounded almost like two because the first shot was almost drowned out by that last squalled "Steve."

Silver had a moment's regret that it had not been his gun that had killed Toledano, but he put that aside. It had been Steve's right.

43

He walked up to Steve. "I'm sorry about the yucca thing," he said. "I didn't ever doubt you. I just had to try to prove—

Steve Donohue shook his head impatiently. "Whatever you could think is all right with me."

They were like two drunks wavering in front of one another, almost too exhausted by torture and by loss of blood to stand.

"It ain't all right," a grim voice said.

They turned to see Jim Clane. Silver had a chance to see that Jim's shoulder wound had been opened during the fight, somehow, but he did not see that Jim had been hit bad in the belly.

"I don't let any man hit me," Jim Clane said, staggering. "Not an' get away with it!"

He hauled off and let Silver have it between the eyes. Silver felt the bone in his nose break before he went staggering back. He did not know how, after six backward steps he kept his feet.

But he did, and, through the red blur that was his vision he could see Jim Clane begin to cry.

"I had to do it," Jim said desperately. "I'll do what he says after this. But I never did let a man bust my nose without bustin' his. Never!"

Beside him, Doc Brimstone roared, "How many times you had your nose busted, Jim?" And broke into laughter.

"Why—only this once," Jim said wonderingly.

Silver grinned. "It's the only time for me, too, Jim. Let's call it square. Except—"

Jim said dully, "Except if I don't obey orders again. I'm sorry, Silver—"

44

"Forget it. I don't need a back-punch in the nose to know a man when I see one!"

Jim looked at Steve Donohue. "Ill say you don't!" he said. And sat down suddenly.

From his low seat he tried to look up at Silver. But Silver also was sitting down. He had managed, by an excess of will, to stay on his feet just half a second longer than Jim....

THE MADNESS OF
SILVER TRENT

THEY WERE putting up a stiffer fight than Trent had looked for. The space behind the ranch house funneled between two buttes, and that was where their line lay—forty or so men spread out in a three hundred yard irregular front—the wicked smashing clamor of their guns close-held and continuous.

Trent lay just in front of the ranch house, his body partly covered by the gradual slope, his chin pressed into the dust, his eyes searching the enemy line before him.

Overhead the bullets whined venomously and close—too close. Behind him he could hear them *thunk* into the adobe walls of the house.

The sharper crack of other rifles sounded to left and right of him as his own crowd returned the fire. He knew that under this hail of lead they had to stick close to cover, taking all their courage and cautious skill to fire at all.

It was one of those places where a man would feel thoroughly licked if he let himself. But Trent could not.

It wasn't just a question of whether they should give back and try to get away. If they gave back, the Bar B X herd would be driven off, and Square Dollar Gaines, who was Trent's friend, would go bust. In a sense, too, the thing was Trent's own fault. He had judged that a bare half dozen of his men would be ample for the job—with what help they might get from Gaines and his three punchers.

That had been a bad miscalculation.

Square Dollar had been in a bad spot from the beginning. He had been losing cattle; he was nearly broke. He had to get this herd to the river and across the border into Texas for the sale he had contracted. And there was a time limit on the deal. Either he got them there in a week or he might just as well not get them there at all.

"Amigo," Trent had grinned. "That's not tough. We'll help you round them up and drive them. More than that, we'll take care of anybody that tries to horn in and make trouble for you. Take it easy."

He owed Gaines his friendship and—if you counted it close enough—his life.

Trent ran his eye again over the enemy line, feeling the anger pushing up in him to threaten his judgment, and which he had to keep continuously fighting back.

It wasn't only that he was being licked. There was something far more. Somehow, this whole set-up smelled. It whispered a name into his mind.

The whole suspicion didn't make sense, and yet…. He steadied himself, grim-jawed. There had to be a way out, and he thought he saw it.

Trent grinned and then cursed himself softly. The opposing line was divided by the terrain into three main sections, expertly disposed to crossfire any attack. But the rises of the ground and the brush would shield a charge from all but the center section.

Shield it until it had gotten into the deeper part of the arroyo, when it would be protected by the arroyo walls.

It was a thing simple and hard to see, but Trent knew that he should have seen it before.

He turned his head toward Magpie Myers, and called,

The rallying cry of Trent's Hawks!
Jim Clane had heard that many
times, but never before had it
sounded so welcome as it did now!

49

"Magpie, pass the word to shoot only at that center bunch. I want 'em fixed so they're afraid to lift a head up. But shoot straight. I want as many of 'em put out of action as I can get."

Magpie nodded, his expression uncomprehending, and Silver turned to repeat the instructions to Doc Brimstone who shot, grunting, on his left.

Doc Brimstone turned his scarlet face with the veins impurpling his nose toward Trent and boomed, "There's not to reason why, Silver. Theirs but to do and be damned!" He grinned and began to bellow the instructions to the left.

Silver grinned in return. Doc was a wonderful drunk and, drunken, a magnificent fighting man. Just as, drunk or sober, he was a superb medico.

An instant later, the fire began to concentrate on the center sector. Silver caught an uplifted head and blasted it out of existence. Somebody else hit a man who lifted suddenly to his full height and then flopped down. The others kept down.

Silver gave the order for his own men to close in toward him. That was the ticklish moment, and the flanks of the enemy, untroubled by return fire, set up a deadly blasting. One of Square Dollar Gaines' punchers lifted to a knee, coughed wetly and sank down. Tonio, a man of Trent's, rolled carefully like a man who knows how to handle himself in a fight and took a random slug in the crown of the head.

TRENT FELT the lump of cold and fighting fury gather in his belly. But after that, the eight of them were almost out of range of the enemy flanks. And the hammering, deadly accuracy of their fire was still concentrated on the center group, who lost two more men.

Then Trent gave his orders. Lars Johanssen, whom bullets sometimes troubled but had never stopped before a charge was over, went first, with Ricardo pacing him. They crawled into the shallow wash, while the others kept the enemy down with a deadly fire.

Then Magpie and Gaines. Then Juan and another Gaines' man. And after them, Trent and another of the Gaines' punchers.

They crawled first on their bellies, then on their hands and knees, then stood erect and ran.

Trent outstripped them all, except Lars, who was too fast and had too much of a start. They hit the arroyo together, and parted, each going to his own side. What followed was something like slaughter.

It appeared that no one there had counted on this. The only warning the enemy had were hurtling figures with blasting sixguns in their hands. And then other figures, parting like marchers in a deadly cotillion. And that was the center bunch.

Panic hit the flanks. Those who escaped the first enfilading blast ran like Hell's scrambling salamanders toward their horses and safety.

Beyond, on the broad flat behind the buttes, the cattle milled, disturbed by this gunfire, but they did not stampede.

When it was over, Trent said, his voice flat, to Gaines: "I reckon that does it. They aren't liable to come back."

Square Dollar said heavily, "Two good men are gone. I reckon you don't figure that keepin' a cowspread from goin' broke is worth all that."

Trent looked at him level-eyed. "Why, no, I can't," he said slowly. "That's one of the things that make it tough. And yet a man's got to make his terms with life. If he can't get those terms met, he's got to hoot and holler until they are, or until he isn't. No man can live forever, not even a coward."

Gaines eyed him somberly. "This wasn't your fight, and you're not takin' it right that a man of yours should die just to see that I ain't busted."

"Not takin' it right!" Trent's eyes flared. "Hombre, leave it lay. We've had plenty of talk about that. I wouldn't like no more."

Square Dollar Gaines took a long breath, and his eyes held sudden regret. "It wasn't worth it, Silver," he said heavily. "No good man's life can be measured in dollars. I—I wish I hadn't let it happen."

Silver Trent looked at 'Tonio's still form, and then he turned a steady gaze on Gaines. "Friend, he said softly. "I've been out of humor, but I reckon 'Tonio wouldn't have been. Like I say, a man has his way to go and his end to meet. An' dollars haven't got anything to do with it. We—"

He stopped suddenly as the hammer of racing hoofs met his ears.

Two horsemen hit the far ridge and catapulted down the long slope. "After a little Silver recognized the lead rider as Pablo. Behind him rode a man tied into his saddle, his head jouncing in the way of one who is near the end of his endurance.

Pablo pulled up, his lean, fanatic face turning toward Silver.

Jefe, "he snarled, "I have brought you an animal to be slaughtered for the coyotes. Read!"

He fumbled in the inner pocket of his charro jacket and drew out a crumpled note. "This dog of dogs had the lack of shame to bring you this," he said. "We were near to killing him back there. But it was thought that you should twist his neck with your own hands. So I have brought him here."

Silver took the note and read it. For a long moment he stood still, with his breath softly indrawn, then he turned and handed it carelessly to Magpie Myers.

"Read it to the boys," he said.

Magpie began to read, slowly with difficulty:

" 'Silver Trent: We have fought one another for a long time. And other people have suffered because of our enmity. I once thought you a Hawk, even though an enemy, but now I think you are only a coyote. Yet even a coyote may fight alone if he is pressed enough. Will you? Let us, then, end our fight on this coming Wednesday.

" 'I will meet you, alone, in the plaza of Los Cuentos, at high noon, to shoot it out with you, man to man. There is no trick. You will walk from the Street on the Twentieth of September, and I from Villa's Street, opposite. Then we'll see who can draw fastest and shoot straightest.

" 'I have sent the word of this challenge around. Will you meet it, coyote?' "

The note was signed, "Esteban Carlos Jaime Juan de los Castillos Bautista y Varro."

Trent's smile was thin. "Well," he said softly, "We've got the message. Turn the messenger loose."

PABLO'S LEAN face blazed into sudden fury. "No, *Jefe!*" he snarled. "No! We have let this messenger of insult and treachery live until you killed him, but if you will not, why I—"

And Pablo's knife flashed in his hand.

"Pablo!" Trent's voice cut like a whip.

Reluctantly, the knife paused, glittering before the terrified messenger's heart.

Trent's men gathered, closing in, their faces grim with the hatred of Esteman Varro—who was known as El Diablo—and of all his renegades.

"No, *Jefe!* Let this one die."

"The fool has dared—let us send him to Hell slowly and as befits him."

"Silver. Why should we—?"

Trent said, *"Basta!* Enough!" And they stood silent while Trent unbound the man and slapped his horse away.

Then Pablo said, stiff and resentful, "Well, *Jefe,* you do as you must do—may the Holy Saints understand it!—but what now of this trap? El Diablo will spread word of his challenge. Surely you are not simple enough to tumble into the snare. It would be strange if we could not be smarter than he."

Trent shrugged, feeling resentment because he remembered that there had been more than one time when only luck and his own quick thinking had gotten him out with his life from one of Esteban Varro's well-laid and deadly traps.

Deep in the core of his mind was an abiding resentment

because a clever man who had neither honor or principle held the advantage over any honest man.

For instance, in this case, Varro could estimate to a fraction of a degree his enemy's reactions. It would be almost impossible for Trent to refuse his challenge, whereas Varro himself would have no conscience about defaulting on his part, and take malicious pleasure in lying in order to trap an honest man.

Yes, perhaps a man was a fool to exercise his honor on a completely dishonorable foeman. Yet Trent couldn't live with himself if he lied, even to a liar; nor if he cheated even a cheat. It was a fatal weakness in a man who could afford no weakness, and who had no other vulnerable spot except the almost equally fatal one of loyalty to his friends.

It was the knowledge of that weakness which sent an intolerable anger blasting through veins and nerves already taut from a bitter day. For an instant his lips were white.

"Shut your damned mouth!" he snarled suddenly at Pablo. "What is it? Have you gotten so you think you can run me now?"

The Mexican's brown face went a grayish-white. His body went rigid. Among Trent's men there was a sudden stunned, ghastly silence as, for a moment, Silver stood glaring out of eyes that were raging gray slits. Then he turned abruptly and stalked away.

Far in the back of his mind was the knowledge that Pablo, at whom he had snarled, had saved his life a dozen times; that he had fought fearlessly by his side in a hundred fights, that he and Magpie Myers were his right and left arms; that....

But this was in the back of his mind. In the front of it, the red tide of his temper held sway. For an instant—for a bare fateful instant—he had the impulse to turn and make an honest and warmhearted apology.

Nothing else would do. Nothing else would heal the wound he had caused. But the impulse came to nothing against the profound storm of his anger against himself and against El Diablo. He walked on, and the moment for that quick, healing apology was lost.

CHAPTER 2
THE CURSE OF HONOR

SILVER RODE a little ahead, his features set and his eyes cold and brooding. On either side, Magpie and Doc Brimstone rode.

Doc Brimstone was almost sober. After the fight the night before, he had drunk up the last of his liquor by way of celebration and also to forget the brooding bitterness in Pablo's eyes. The result in this hot noon was that his breath came in audible gasps.

The sound irritated Silver.

The temper he had had the evening before had carried over through the night and the next morning. With the dawn he had recognized his own guilt and known what he must try to do to win Pablo back to him.

For it was not merely Pablo he had alienated, he knew—it was also the rest of his men. Their eyes avoided a direct meeting with his and when he surprised them looking at him their gaze was strange and obscurely questioning.

Maybe it was the knowledge of his own fault that stiffened him into a false pride, or maybe it was the continued run of his own helpless anger. In any case, he said nothing to Pablo until after he had chosen Magpie and Doc to ride with him. Then, crisp and cold-eyed, he left Pablo in charge of the men remaining at the ranch.

"Nothing will happen," he had said, thin-lipped, "but you might as well stay here until Square Dollar can move the herd on across the Border.

"I'll be back maybe day after tomorrow, but Thursday morning at the latest," Trent had then said to Square Dollar Gaines. "It'll be time enough to begin the drive then."

Square Dollar nodded. "Time enough, an' not too much," he said bleakly.

When Silver's eyes showed a sudden blaze, the ranchman said, swiftly placating, "No complaint. You've helped me plenty an' I won't forget it. Now you've got somethin' you got to do an'—I plumb understand how you feel. Besides, the trouble here's over. Thursday we'll start the drive. Good luck to you, Trent. I wish you'd let me go along with you. You ain't takin' enough men."

Trent knew that he wasn't, but his idea was to go into town and find out what the situation was, ask a few questions, try to find out just what El Diablo's trap was. Then, if the challenge was honest, he would meet it—with whatever protection seemed necessary.

As he rode, he regretted his choice of men. It would have been better, of course, to have Pablo along, and with him, Ricardo. But Pablo had been impossible of course, and the hurt and wondering look in Ricardo's eyes had been too much for Silver to endure. Silver's public and unnecessary affront to Pablo had struck deep at Ricardo.

The low, gray huddle of the Mexican town in the distance added nothing to his peace of mind. He felt suddenly unsure of himself. But no one in Los Cuentos would have known that, seeing him ride in.

Along the streets, talk of the townsfolk died suddenly at his appearance and then buzzed up audibly when the trio was past. It was like walking through a lane of flies that held silent as he passed and then buzzed up behind him an instant later.

The first cantina told him that the Varro's challenge was public knowledge.

"This time," the *patrón* said, wiping some of the permanent stickiness off the bar in his excitement, "this time Señor Varro has made a mistake. The Señor Halcon—the Hawk—will kill him swiftly. All the town knows this and waits for it."

Magpie eyed him coldly. "But this Varro never wanted to face Silver before. Hombre," he drawled in Spanish, "what is all this—a trick?"

The *patrón's* eyes blazed. "I would like to see it, señor," he squeaked. "There is not a man, woman or child in this town that does not want to see Señor Seelver kill this—this...."

He sobered suddenly, realizing how his life was in jeopardy

by talking so against the greatest power in that section of the country. But then he shrugged.

"There is no chance of a trick, señor," he said calmly. "If there was a trick, neither Señor Varro nor any of his men would leave this town alive!"

Everywhere that night and the next day, there was the same story. The townspeople were afraid of Esteban Varro, but their hearts were with Silver. They knew the long feud between Silver and Varro, and they saw now that the end of it was at hand with victory, they felt sure, for the Hawk of the Sierras. For who could draw with Silver's lightning speed, or shoot with his deadly accuracy?

No. It would be over on Wednesday at noon, and there would be no treachery, for if Silver Trent were shot down from the side or from behind, Los Cuentos would tear Varro limb from limb and flay the rest of his shameless men, until they called on their God, vainly and impiously before their souls fled to Hell.

SILVER LOOKED at Magpie Myers and got no more than a puzzled shake of the head from him. Doc Brimstone, who had finally recovered from his ride with the aid of half a dozen double tequilas, looked at him and grinned.

"You're certainly the favorite of the Gods of Los Cuentos," he grinned jovially. "I don't see how even Varro can think up an answer to that. He's no fool. He wouldn't try anything here. Or would he?"

Silver chewed his lower lip reflectively. "Damn' if I know," he murmured. "Anyway, we'll find out tomorrow noon."

"You're gonna meet him here, with only the two of us to back yuh?" Magpie demanded slowly.

"You two ought to be enough."

Magpie looked grim. "Mebbe. But from where I sit it looks plumb foolhardy."

"You'd want me to quit an' run out with my tail between my legs."

Magpie shook his head somberly. "Yuh can't do that," he grated. "Was you to run, that would be the end of El Halcon in all Mexico. There wouldn't be anybody to take a coward in, or any hole for his men to run to. You—an' us—would be finished."

Silver's smile was swift and warm. "Right, old timer! And so we stay. If there's a trick, it's me they want and it's me they'll get first. So let's let it go at that!"

It was midnight, Tuesday, when they drifted into Juan Reyes' cantina, and found Joselito there.

Joselito stood maybe five feet three in good high boots, and he was all bantam. When Silver came in he swept off his tall straw sombrero and his eyes blazed.

"Señor," he cried, *"Buenas tardes!* Permit me, Joselito—who is nobody—to welcome you and to beg you the honor drinking with me."

Silver felt the silence fall on the cantina, a little shocked that anyone, not knowing him, should call out so to Silver Trent, *El Halcon de los Sierras.*

With the swift perception of men and motives which had helped him become, in his way, a great leader of men, he understood Joselito and spoke to him as he should have been spoken to. He had no thought of refusing, but also he did not bow or follow the formal tone which this small defiant man had invited. Instead, he spoke like a friend.

"Amigo," he said simply, "The honor is mine. I will drink with you gladly."

It was as though a sigh of relief mingled with astonishment had run through the room.

Joselito's chest swelled like that of a small rooster about to crow. "Don Seelver's pleasure," he snapped at Juan Reyes, who stared bug-eyed from behind the bar. "And that of the *caballeros* with him!"

It did not take any prophet to know that Joselito's grandchildren would hear of this incident.

Silver raised his glass. *"Salud y pesetas, señor.* Tell me, are you the Joselito of whom one hears as a matador on his way to greatness?"

The bantam's eyes flashed with pride. "The Hawk does me too much honor," he cried. "I am but a poor amateur, not worthy to be mentioned with the great Joselito whose name I humbly bear. I but stumble in his footsteps."

Silver said gravely, "All skills are hard to learn. For fame, talent and courage are required, together with long hard work. In the first two, report has it, you are rich. The last is with yourself, and time."

The inflation went out of Joselito's chest but in its place another kind of pride grew visibly. It was plain to see the thing work in him, without vanity, with the sudden, overwhelming sobriety a squire of olden times might have felt when the sword touched his shoulder and the voice said, "Arise, Sir Knight."

"Señor," Joselito said, hardly breathing,, "a man of no consequence, like myself, may dare to face a bull with what skill he has. That is nothing. It is you who are the great matador. Not one of us—unlike yourself—has ever dared to face the Devil who is more subtle and more savage and more dangerous than any bull."

A gasp ran through the room as men heard El Diablo thus named openly and without respect. But Joselito's voice went on without tremor. "Yet tomorrow you face him, and all that he may do or contrive. But señor, even that is little. If you were to die, still we who have looked on your face would be proud, because we have lived in the same world with you!"

Trent felt the tiredness and the doubt go out of him. He understood that he'd have a hundred watchful protectors against treachery tomorrow; and that if he lost, it would not really matter. He would be dead, but what he had stood for would live on, and there would be other men and other fighters....

He, Silver Trent—bandit and branded murderer was only an incident in man's fight toward decency. That perception and that humility was in him, tightening his throat as he faced this bantam man.

He found it hard to speak and his expression was moved and humble. He said at last, softly, "A man's honor is his own, amigo. But what it wins for him or loses for him is his own also. It has been a happiness to meet you."

Afterwards, at the hotel, the memory of the crowds' sudden spontaneous cheer as he walked out of the cantina, and of

Joselito's words and his eyes were still with him, stronger than anything else.

But Magpie growled sourly, "Shore! Awful purty an' touchin'. If El Diablo had of been there, he'd of likely bust out cryin'. But seein' he wasn't, it don't say there ain't shenanigans afoot."

Silver grinned. "Maybe not," he said. "What do you say we get some sleep?"

THE KNOCK on Silver's door brought him awake all over, like a man popped up from some great depth by a sudden explosion. He lay for a split second with his nerves throbbing and then got out of bed. The movement of it was panther-soft and fast. He pulled open the door.

"You can put the gun away," Pablo said stiffly, standing in the hallway, his voice over-courteous.

Silver slid the .45 onto the dresser and lit the lamp.

In its light he saw that the stiffness of Pablo's voice and carriage was that of a man holding himself together by sheer physical strength.

There was a dark splotch on Pablo's shirt which had seeped through the charro jacket he wore.

Trent took one look at it and at Pablo's face. Then he said, "Get on the bed, man! What happened? Who shot you, amigo?"

Pablo said, stiffly polite, "I don't need to get on a bed, thank you. Señor Gaines and his daughter have been taken, and the herd has been driven off."

Having said that, his knees buckled and he fell on his face on the floor, the sound of his forehead on the planks coming sharply in the silence.

Silver picked him up and put him on the bed, feeling somehow as if it had been his own head which had bounced on the floor. Then he went out into the hall and down to where Magpie and Doc Brimstone shared a room.

Doc Brimstone stumbled down the hall groaning and cursing. When he saw Pablo his curses deepened and speeded up.

"What are you standing there for?" he bellowed at Magpie. "Go and get my bag."

He bent over Pablo and began taking the clothing from over his wound with fingers that might have handled a moth's wing without disturbing its delicate dust.

After Magpie brought his instruments, he probed for the bullet and then straightened with the slug in his hand. "Missed his lung and lodged against the shoulder blade," he bellowed. "The fool's too lucky for this world. But that's the only thing that'll keep him from livin'."

Then he whirled on Silver, poking a pudgy unsurgeonly finger at him. "Why in hell didn't you shoot him dead instead of sayin' what you—" He broke off abruptly. "All right," he bawled, red-faced. "I know you're sorry for it."

He swung on Magpie, roaring, "Get whisky and hot water! Or are you too damn' old to move."

Magpie moved, glowering. But Silver stood still. His lean, hard-bitten face had drawn into a grim, etched mask. Only his eyes were alive, brooding, hurt and full of growing cold fury.

Doc Brimstone stared at him uneasily.

"Aw, Silver," he mumbled, "don't take it that way. I—"

Trent's full, sudden stare cut him off. "Don't you see it?" he asked.

Doc Brimstone looked puzzled.

"This was Varro's game," Silver went on, his voice flat. "This was why he challenged me. Those hombres that we fought back at Square Dollar's ranch were not *supposed* to win! And when we thought they had lost, and Gaines' herd was safe, I was supposed to get Varro's challenge.

"Everybody else in Mexico got it at the same time. Everybody in this whole town knew about it before we got here. He knew I wouldn't be fool enough not to come in an' look the lay of the land before the fight, and he fixed it so that his men would strike when I was gone—really strike this time. *Because he didn't ever intend to shoot it out with me!*

"He knew well I'd help my friend, and to hell with the challenge. And so he can strut and say that I had been afraid to meet him, and that would be the end of me, just as definitely as though he had put a bullet in me."

Doc Brimstone's face purpled. "Why, curse it, if you knew that—!"

"I didn't," Silver said grimly.

"But you've got to meet him, man!"

"I—I can't!"

MAGPIE, WITH whisky in one hand and boiling water in the other, froze. "Look, Silver," he said hoarsely, "You can't do that. If you do, it means you're finished! All of us! Didn't you hear that little Joselito tonight. These folks *believe* in you, man! Show yellow to them an' they'll turn against us to a man.

65

There won't be a hole small enough for us to crawl into. And any witless peon that has a gun will think he's good enough to shoot us in the back."

"Still we're riding to help Gaines," Silver said through stiff lips.

From the bed, Pablo groaned. But when he spoke his thin voice was cold and too polite. And still he did not call Silver *"Jefe."*

Señor," he said, and the word made Trent wince almost visibly. "Señor, if you are not here at noon tomorrow, you had better ride straight for the Border and keep riding. I say this because I know my people."

Silver looked at him and his eyes narrowed. "You'd have me leaves Gaines and his daughter to get along the best way they can?"

"Neither is your father or your mother, señor," Pablo said coldly. "If you want to help them, you can do so—but do it after tomorrow noon."

"And if I kill Varro, they will die. He'll have given orders for that."

Pablo merely looked at him.

Silver's eyes narrowed. "Do you, by any chance, think I am yellow?"

Pablo's face was cold. His shoulders shrugged slightly. "Men change, señor," he said warily. "That has been seen and known before. Go with God."

The color drained slowly and completely out of Trent's face. He looked at Doc Brimstone, who avoided his eyes. And then at Magpie who said, hard-voiced, "A lot of folks are dependin' on you here, Silver."

That was true. But it was the memory of Joselito that came to Silver and stabbed him—Joselito who was brave and who could be braver if Silver justified Joselito's worshipping faith in him.

And yet he had to let Joselito down, along with the others. It was a sudden agony inside him. He was going out like a thief in the night, with no word to any man, no explanation. There were only nine hours between him and his meeting with El Diablo. How could he explain why he would not wait?

The lines of his face were deep-etched as wordlessly he caught up his gun-belts and stalked from the room.

In the corral of the livery barn he found his horse, saddled him and rode.

At the edge of town he pulled up and looked back. The place was dark and silent under the light of a thin moon, whitewashed dobe glinting dim in black shadow. The scent of *Dama del Noche* drifted to him with its faint sweetness.

He spoke softly to Joselito, who slept in one of those moon-bathed adobes. "I didn't know exactly how important it was then, amigo," he murmured. "But a man's honor is his own. It belongs to him and no one else. I hope you don't have to learn it like I have—the hard way."

He turned then and rode on.

CHAPTER 3
AT HELL'S HACIENDA

MIDWAY ON the way to Gaines ranch, he turned off abruptly, his lips flat and his eyes smouldering with the anger and the hurt that had ridden him all the way from Los Cuentos.

The fact was, he knew now, the men who had ridden with him for years had deserted him. Pablo, Doc Brimstone, Magpie…. Back at the ranch, he would find Lars and the others and maybe they would desert him too. Well, he didn't need them—didn't want them!

Even the thought of seeing Magpie, Pablo or Doc again was something that he could not face. And to say a hating or contemptuous word to them would be something he could not stand. Everything may be borne except the defection of a friend. And when that happens, it must be taken in silence.

Silver Trent was used to loneliness because he was a man who led men. And that is a lonely job. But he had led men who trusted him and were behind him every moment—even when he rode without them. And so the loneliness had sometimes been burdensome but it had never hurt. This time, he was wholly alone.

Riding so, the country took on a new aspect to him, seemed strange and more forbidding than he had ever known it. It oppressed him, the hot, blank blue glare of the sky and the harsh, barren rocks of the hills, with the cactus stunted and the twisted saguaros thrusting up rachitic arms as though supplicating the sun to beat down less harshly.

He had figured out—or thought he had—what Varro would have done with Square Dollar and his girl. He thought he knew where to find them.

In the subtle and deadly chess game whose opening gambits had been El Diablo's, he believed now, grimly, that he had thought of a move that Varro had not foreseen.

There wasn't any doubt but that Varro's men had had orders to bring Gaines and his daughter to Esteban Varro's own home rancho. And there wasn't any doubt that he, Silver, was supposed to follow, raging, with his men. Maybe Varro thought that he would deviate from the straight trail, to go by his hideout and collect the rest of the gang. Maybe Varro hoped for this and had laid his plans for that kind of trap. But certainly, Varro believed that Silver would go first to the Gaines rancho, in order to pick up the trail. Silver was certain of that because that is what he would ordinarily have done, and so he knew Varro would judge him that way.

But he couldn't be smart enough to know that Silver would feel himself alone and desperate, and thus willing to gamble everything on a hunch. There were plenty of places that El Diablo's men might be holding Gaines and the girl. But Silver chose one and rode that way.

At noon he stopped for lunch, regretting that he had been angry enough to forget to take anything with him. His lunch consisted of slicing a barrel cactus and drinking the water that was in it. That was after he had taken care of his horse in the same way. Then he rode on.

The second day found him and the horse gaunt, and with their lips cracking.

That was the day after what had happened in Los Cuentos. Silver hadn't needed anything to tell him about that. He could see El Diablo riding arrogantly out into the square and pretending to be surprised at not finding his cowardly adversary there. He had made a speech probably. And Joselito—if he had not cut his own throat—had at least wanted to. He shook his head, refusing to think of it. El Diablo, if Silver's guess was right, had started for home instantly after that planned fiasco in the town. He would know by then that Silver had taken the bait and would come roaring up soon or late, with his men behind him, to take back Gaines and the girl.

But he would figure on Silver coming a little later than Silver intended. And that was the one chance he had to keep alive.

The horse couldn't go any more on that mid-afternoon of the third day. It was hotter than it should have been, even in this season, and Silver had miscalculated by a good five miles on how much the horse could stand.

HE FOUGHT and pled with him before he could get the gelding on his feet and over to the meager shade of some grease-wood growing against the face of a rock that began nowhere and ended in nothing. And he sought and found water cactus for him before he staggered off on his own way.

The five miles to the pass were the longest Silver had ever traveled. He had had little water and no food for three days of riding almost without rest. And this way to the entrance of the slit between two great rock walls which hemmed in El Diablo's hacienda was over pure badlands. There, the glass-rock cut his boots and his hands and arms like razor blades when he fell.

He hoped that there would be only one guard. And lying flat on the sharp rocks with the sun lowering, he could see only one. The fellow moved lazily, smoked, drank wine from a goatskin, but he gave no evidence of being off-guard. And the way down was almost devoid of cover.

Silver took it crawling. His tongue stuck in the top of his mouth and he could not sweat. For moments on end the scarlet cloud that had intermittently obscured his vision came down to make him almost blind.

He was almost a hundred yards away when the guard saw him. And that was too far.

The man's head jerked up suddenly and the rifle in his hands leaped to his shoulder. In the same instant, he turned his head a little, yelling to somebody back in the canyon.

Then he leveled his rifle at Silver and said, "Stand up, you!" in Spanish.

Silver sighted the sixgun carefully and shot, once. The guard's rifle went off in the same instant, the bullet kicking rock splinters into Silver's face. Then the man buckled at the knees and went down.

Silver got up and began to run. Crashing down hill he hit the mouth of the canyon just as two other Varro guards hit a bend in the canyon about twenty yards away.

They were quick. The first man flung up his rifle and slammed a quick shot at Silver, while the other dived behind rocks. Silver shot the first man fast, his lead from the hip deadly at that short range. Then he shot at the man behind the rocks.

And as he shot he began to run forward. It was his only chance. There was no cover for him here. He had to go forward or run back, with almost a certainty of being shot in the spine.

But he had this advantage. The man was behind rock, and that is bad cover. Silver shot as he ran, his slugs clipping rock, the flying slivers almost as deadly as the lead itself.

El Diablo's man came up, crouching, his gun blasting, just as Silver loomed over the rocks. His lead caught Silver just in the angle of the shoulder, high enough only to crease him deeply. And then Silver's right hand Colt hammered three times, and the man fell face down on the rocks....

In a small brush corral near the canyon's other entrance he found three horses. He picked the best of them and then led him back to the bodies of the three guards.

One of them was bigger than most Mexicans, and wore a sombrero with a jaguar-skin band ornamented by big cut-steel buckle.

Silver drew a deep breath. The buckle would flash like fire in the late sun. He had a chance, even though those at El Diablo's hacienda had heard the shooting.

He took the hat for his own and realized by a quick comparison of stirrups that it was the hat-owner's horse he had chosen. He rode into the hacienda yard at a dead run.

The four men who ran out to meet him did not recognize him

in time. Silver shot one in the shoulder and another square in the head just as they raised their guns to shoot.

The other two did better. One bullet hit Silver's horse and sent him and his rider hurtling and sliding to the ground.

Silver managed to roll with the fall and hang onto the gun in his hand, but the breath was knocked out of him and he could not use his weapon.

The second of the two shot fast four times, but the first bullet hit the heel of Trent's boot, knocking it off. The second cut a slice from his leg, the third missed, going into the gravel behind him. But the fourth was a paralyzing blow in his side.

It was only then that he was able to shoot, in that moment before the paralysis hit him. A small blue bruise jumped into the second man's forehead—a curious bruise, ringed by red before his face hit the ground.

The gun had dropped from Trent's hand then while the paralysis of his right side began. And the man who was still alive saw that. He was a squat, pockmarked man with small cruel eyes, and now he walked forward slowly.

Silver was looking up at him, still not quite able to move. He saw the gun-muzzle level, looked into its gaping mouth, knowing that the slug would hit him squarely in the forehead.

The gaping muzzle held him there, with a kind of numbed curiosity and fascination, so that he saw the object that sailed through the air only as a quick blur.

It must have hit the Mexican's head a split second before his gun went off, for the slug missed.

A little, slowly, a little dazed, Silver struggled to his feet.

In the doorway of the hacienda, the pallid, oval face of Betty Gaines, Square Dollar's daughter, showed. The Varro man groaned a little and began to move. Silver clipped him behind the ear with the barrel of his sixgun and went on toward the house. He leaned against one of the piazza pillars.

"How'd you get loose?" he asked her, with a polite, formal air which he felt was out of place.

"You're hurt," she said looking at him from wide eyes.

"I asked you a question," Silver said severely.

She looked at him as though he were a little insane. "They— they let me loose," she stammered. "They thought I was harmless."

Silver looked back at the small bronze statue of Mephistopheles which lay beside the unconscious Mexican who had been about to kill him.

"Their mistake," he said gravely, with an air of gallantry. "No lady is ever quite harmless."

She stared at him from her dilated eyes, and for a moment swayed as though she would faint.

"Are there any others around?" Silver inquired politely.

"No. At least I don't think so," she said breathlessly. "Most of them rode off this morning. There are only some servants— peons. Dad—" She drew in a slow breath. "Dad is—"

"Yes," Silver said with decision. "There's your father. We must see to him."

He stumbled going in, and went down to his knees.

The movement seemed to shock him into some kind of

normality. He drew a long breath and said, "Look, I've been hit a little. Do you think you could find me a drink?"

HE HAD come completely out of his bullet-shock by the time Square Dollar, the girl and himself got back to the canyon. At the other end they saw movement, faint and flickering on the trail above.

"Inside here!" Silver snapped.

They took cover just within the canyon's mouth and waited.

Four riders trotted down the trail, and one of them was dressed all in black, with a cloak which covered the twisted hunch of his back—El Diablo!

Silver drew in his breath softly.

Varro and his men rode down a quick run on tired horses which yet could take a pace. In this late, soft light, Silver could see the dust and sweat on them. And now one of them rode ahead, as though it were a customary thing and yelled carelessly, *"Ola!"*

Silver tried to remember the voice of the first guard who had yelled, and he called out *"Ola!"*

The man rode on looking a little surprised and frowning, so that Silver knew that somehow he had made a mistake. The others drew up sharply, at El Diablo's gesture.

Silver made his voice suddenly drunken. *"Ola! Ola! Ola!"* he yelled. *"Salud y pesetas, hombre! Que pasa?* Have you fear?"

They came on then and El Diablo's eyes had death in them for a drunken servant.

Silver said, with his guns in his hands, "Try to move a little señores. I wish it very much—*yo lo quiero mucho.*"

Maybe it was the tone of his voice as much as the guns in his and Gaines' hands that kept them from moving.

Silver was sick but he saw the fear and the pale fury in El Diablo's eyes as they bound them all. And it was something that he would remember.

They left the other three there, but Silver took El Diablo with him.

"Why don't you kill him?" Square Dollar asked. "Are you too soft to kill a murderer?"

Silver shook his head. "I need him," he said softly. "I need him alive."

CHAPTER 4
BONDS OF FIGHTING BLOOD

LOS CUENTOS was dead that noon, under heat that lay on the town like a blight. But nobody cared about the heat. Because there was another kind of blight that had made men's hearts small within them.

Joselito sat in the dim front room of his small adobe house. His wife came to him desperately. "Do something!" she cried. "Eat something! You have to live. You can't sit there forever. Have you no sense? Because a bandit turns out to be—"

Joselito got up slowly from his chair and turned tortured eyes on his wife. "Woman," he said slowly, fingering his knife. "I am not much of a man. I obey you in all things. But, please, I ask you—"

The woman's face paled. "Joselito!" she cried. "I but love you. I did not mean—"

She broke off as her husband got up from his chair, signaling for silence. There was the thud of hoofs on the street.

He walked to the window, and drew in one long slow breath. *"Dios!"* he said softly. *"Dios mio!"*

"What is it, Joselito?"

He drew himself up like a bantam. "Shut up, woman," he said with the voice coming great and proud out of his chest. "Go to your kitchen where you belong. There is man's work a-foot."

"Joselito! Are you crazy?"

"Silence!"

She shrank back from him as he stalked out of the house.

He was not the only man who had seen that passage. The town buzzed with it. And there was audience enough when Silver and his captive got to the great square.

Silver was gaunt and lean, his clothes worn and dusty, but there was a lift in his voice and a fire in his eyes that held men, that drew them, edging closer to the crackle of his words.

"Friends," he began, "most of you heard about the challenge this dog, Varro, issued to me to meet him here. And all of you know that I didn't come.

"I expect that some of you were disappointed. You thought I was yellow. You had believed in me, and I had failed you. But if I had come here to save my outward honor, I would have had to fail in a deeper obligation, to a friend.

"Varro knew that. He never intended to fight it out with me. He arranged to make the kind of trouble for my friend that would take me away from here just at the time I was supposed to be here to fight him. He wanted me to seem yellow, to discredit me with you. Because he thought that if you were not my friends he would find it easier to win his old fight with me—a fight that he has carried on by cunning, by treachery, by lies and bribery and murder and every kind of dishonor. It's not for nothing that he is called El Diablo—the Devil!"

A mutter ran through the crowd that grew into a sudden excited shout, that carried a note of savagery in it.

Silver stilled it with a lifted hand.

"When I had gotten through with the business that took me away," he went on, "I was at some trouble to go and pull this fox out of his hole and bring him here. I didn't want you, amigos, to miss your fun!"

The crowd broke out in frenzied cheering. Men slapped one another on the back and tossed their hats in the air. But Joselito, standing like a blazing-eyed bantam on the edge of the inner circle, cried out fiercely.

"Is it for a man to fight a dog? Give him to us, Silver, and we'll tear the hide from him and hang him more naked than he was born!"

A great yell answered that and the crowd surged forward.

Varro, still tied to his horse, shrank, his face paling to a bloodless yellow.

Silver's voice stopped them. "Stand back!" he shouted. "Do you want to dishonor me again?" His eyes shown wolfishly. "Señor Varro's hands have not once been tied during our ride together. I didn't want him to be able to say that he didn't have enough circulation in them, so he couldn't use his guns. And I've brought them, too." He held up a pair of gold embossed Colts for the crowd to see.

He cut Varro loose and handed the six-shooters to him.

"Look at them and see that they are properly loaded. I'm going to give you every chance Varro, and then I'm going to rid the earth of you for good. I'm going to kill you so dead that you'll stink in hell! Get down off that horse!"

Stiffly, Varro obeyed, his hunched form seeming a symbol of black hatred, his narrowed, venomous eyes shuttling this way and that as though seeking some way of escape, or some help among that hostile crowd."

"Clear two lanes—one behind me and one behind Varro," Silver called, and waited while the crowd broke and moved, leaving the lanes clear, except for one man who stood directly behind Varro. That was Joselito.

"I take my chances, Silver," he yelled fiercely. "You are too careless with this crawling scorpion. If there is treachery here, I will have my knife in the hunch of his back before he can bat an eyelash."

Silver shook his head. "Back! This is between Varro and me."

Reluctantly, Joselito gave back, sliding his knife back into his belt. But he continued to be in the line of fire.

"*Joselito!* Get to one side. You will be shot." That was Joselito's wife, who ran frantically out behind Silver.

And Silver turned his head. It was the one mistake that Esteban Varro was waiting for.

"Get out of—" Silver said quickly to Joselito's wife, and as he

79

spoke, Varro's hands moved. They moved too fast for the yell of warning to burst from the crowd.

Even so, Silver spun, and the flick of his gun out of its holster was like the lightning flick of a lizards' tongue.

Too late, by a tenth of a second. The crashing explosion of Varro's guns drowned out the crowd's belated yell. One slug snarled harmlessly by, but the other took Silver in the shoulder and slammed him to the ground.

Varro ran like a crouching cat and whipped into the saddle. His spurred horse jumped for the space between the crowd, whirled, and was out of shooting range.

Wearily Silver got to his feet. He knew there was no chance of overtaking Varro before he got back to his guarded hacienda.

He had failed again. Joselito's small excited figure burst through the crowd towing an immense rotund form behind him.

"Sit down you fool!" Doc Brimstone bellowed.

SILVER GRINNED faintly. He didn't know from where Doc Brimstone had appeared but the rolling gait and scarlet face assured him that it was Doc, and that was enough.

"Sit down and lie down before I knock you down!" Doc Brimstone boomed.

Silver hadn't had any intention of sitting down, but the weariness in him acted as though it had a will of its own. His knees buckled and he found himself sitting foolishly on the rough paving of the square.

Doc Brimstone's big fat hand shoved him down on his back with an odd gentleness. Then his big blunt fingers began to probe at the wound.

"Missed the bone," he muttered, "you have the luck of—God's pajamas! You're already shot to doll-rags. What foolishness have you been up to now?" He bellowed savagely at Joselito. "What are you standing around for? Get men to carry him to bed!"

Abruptly a blown horse raced into the square, his sliding shoes striking sparks from the stone slabs.

A gray-faced figure flung himself from the saddle and staggered towards Silver, the crowd parting before him. It was Magpie Meyers.

"I lost you," Magpie said, "because I'm a fool. I thought sure you would go to the ranch. But I found the herd. Silver, we can get it! Come on…." He stopped, his fatigued eyes focusing for the first time. "Hombre, you're hurt!

Silver sat up, despite Doc Brimstone's outraged bellow. His eyes looked dazed.

"You found the cattle? But you said—"

"When are you going to get some sense," Magpie yelled at him.

Silver stared at him unbelieving for a minute before the weight inside him lightened and disappeared, as though a stone had evaporated. For he knew Magpie—none of them—had borne him any resentment. They had only fought blindly to save his personal reputation.

He got to his feet in one movement, but the red mist came into his mind again and he staggered and nearly fell.

He caught himself, and weaved toward his horse.

"Come on," he snapped at Magpie, "let's ride."

"Not without me, *Jefe!*" a voice called, and men fell away

81

before a lean gaunt man who seemed to burn his way through the crowd with the flame of his own eyes. It was Pablo.

"That man kept me in bed, *Jefe!*" he said, pointing a lean finger at Doc Brimstone.

"And that's where you're going now!" Doc yelled, red-faced. "And this imbecile with you!"

Pablo turned his burning gaze on Joselito. "Get me a horse, amigito, and very quickly," he said softly, "lest I strip the skin from your small body!"

Joselito's eyes blazed back at him. "But quickly señor," he breathed, "two are saddled there at the corner of the square. One for me and one for you. I don't know who owns them, but whoever it is will gladly lend them." He touched the knife in his belt significantly. "Very gladly, indeed," he said.

Silver and Magpie swung into their saddles while Pablo and Joselito ran for the horses.

A moment later they were hammering out of the square while Doc Brimstone stood red-faced and bellowed profanity.

The crowd stood silent, a look of wonder, almost of awe on the brown faces until Doc Brimstone's infuriated roar got through to them. "Get me a horse, you gaping fools! You expect me to get one myself?"

CHAPTER 5
DEATH PLAYS ITS HAND

A T SQUARE DOLLAR GAINES' ranch, Jim Clane and the others of Silver's Hawks waited grim-faced. After staring at the ground, Jim shook himself and repeated stubbornly, "I say we have to go after them now."

Lars Johanssen shook his head with equal stubbornness, "Magpie said to vait," he said, "so ve vait."

Sudden temper stained Jim's cheeks. "The hell with what Magpie said," he snapped. "Gaines hadn't come in then. Accordin' to him, Silver is hurt bad. By the time he gets through finishin' off Varro he won't be fit to ride. Pablo's laid up. So who are we waiting for? Magpie? That's only one man and those hombres are liable to start movin' the cattle any time. Mebbe we can't wipe 'em out, but we can hold 'em where they are until we can get the rest of the gang."

Lars shook his head. "Magpie says vait, so ve vait," he rumbled, but there was a note of doubt in his voice.

Square Dollar Gaines cut in, "never mind the cattle," he said savagely, "I've been broke before, I'm not getting anybody else killed over a few dollars' worth of dumb cows."

Betty Gaines applauded softly. "The herd has done enough harm, Dad," she said. "Let them go; we'll get along somehow."

One of Square Dollar's punchers stirred. "It ain't that," he said, "but there's more than twenty of them hombres. We ain't got a chance."

Jim Clane got to his feet and faced them with his jaw jutting. "The hell you preach!" he snarled. "What are you anyway? Yellow? This is something we started. Do you think Silver would quit on it?"

His hands fell to the butts of the twin guns. "I'm ridin' out, and I'm ridin' out now," he blazed. "Is anybody with me?"

Lars Johanssen lumbered to his feet. "You call me yellow?" he demanded reddening.

Jim's eyes narrowed, "I'm not calling you," he said. "I'm just askin'." And there was a sure amusement in his voice.

Lars grinned suddenly. "You dern redheaded hellion," he rumbled. "C'mon, let's get going."

Jim Clane's body relaxed. His voice took on a tone of leadership. "That makes it easy," he said, "somebody has got to stay here with Miss Gaines and Square Dollar, it had better be you. The rest of us will go on. Mebbe we can't lick 'em, but we can keep 'em plenty busy until somebody shows up. Hit saddles, men!"

Square Dollar Gaines' face hardened. "Betty can stay alone. You're not going without me!"

The girl's blue eyes flashed. "And you're not going without me, either," she said. "I can shoot as well as any man here."

Her father looked from her back at Jim Clane. "No use to argue," he said, pride in his voice. "When she talks that-away, there's nothin' to be done about it."

Magpie followed easily the sign of the herd. He circled the cliff around the valley and reported that Varro's crowd had not even bothered to post guards. Evidently Varro had counted on the abduction of Gaines and his daughter to occupy the whole attention of Trent's men.

Jim led them to the open edge of the valley. From there they had a view of the herd, closely held by three riders. The rest of Varro's men were hunkered down by a small fire under the out-shelving wall of one of the side cliffs.

Their reason for not having guards was evident at once. There was a clear three hundred yards between the edge of the scrub oak which bordered the valley entrance and the herd. Between was clear grass land without cover.

Jim Clane breathed a sigh of satisfaction. "The fools," he exclaimed, "have run themselves into a trap. All we got to do is hold them here!"

And as he spoke, a rider appeared on the far rim of the valley. He sat his horse there a moment, looking downward at the scene before him, making a queer, hunched black figure against the clear evening sky.

Jim Clane caught his breath and swore unbelievingly. "Varro," he whispered. "Hell, it ain't possible." As he spoke the rider dipped suddenly below the valley rim.

Later, Jim and the others heard his voice ring out in command. The men under the cliffside raced for their horses while the riders with the herd began moving the cattle.

Jim Clane galvanized into action. "They're taking 'em out the other end," he said. "Gaines, you take one man and your girl and guard this side. We'll go around and trap 'em in that canyon."

Followed by the others, he spurred away.

The gang below had broken into two groups, one following the herd and the other ahead with Varro. Jim could see that Varro was excitedly urging the drag riders to get the herd moving at a fast pace.

At the far corner of the valley, Jim swung left and almost plunged down over the side of a hidden canyon which was concealed by heavy brush.

"This does it," he said softly, "We've got 'em bottled up."

He whipped his Winchester out of the saddle boot and sighted it on the leading Varro rider. The thin, wicked crack of the rifle split the evening quiet, and a Varro man plunged sideways to the ground from his saddle.

At once, the oncoming riders, three seconds after the report of the Winchester, had left their saddles and were diving for what scanty cover the level floor of the valley afforded. Almost instantly their answering lead began to search the mouth of the canyon.

Behind them the herd checked, milling.

Immediately the ten or dozen men who were with Varro in the rear surged forward, yelling. Whipped on by Varro's savage commands, they raced straight for the canyon mouth.

Jim Clane caught his breath softly. "The fools!" he muttered. "They're going to try to rush us." He turned to the men behind him. "Leave Varro for me," he said. "He's mine."

Behind him, Lars Johanssen grunted, "That's what you think. I haf something for that hombre, myself!"

But Varro kept carefully in the rear of his charging men. When he drew almost level with the line that had dismounted, he flung himself from the saddle and took cover, while his shrill cry urged the others forward.

It was that line, firing from cover, which gave the charging horsemen their chance. As they hurtled closer towards the canyon mouth, the fire from the first group intensified, so that the opening was swept by an almost solid hail of lead.

Jim Clane and Lars fired methodically, oblivious to the vicious whine of lead around their ears. The others kept cover, ducking out only for hurried shots, so that it was only the deadly fire of Jim and Lars that finally broke the charge.

Three saddles were empty before the Varro men slowed. Then a bullet of Jim Clane's took the horse of the leading rider squarely in the forehead. The animal went down as though pole-axed. His hind legs flinging sideways so that the horses of the two following riders piled into him and went down in a scrambling, squealing mass.

The others pulled up and ran for it.

Jim Clane looked at Lars and grinned. "We can do that every-day in the week," he said. "And twice on Sunday."

Lars' answering grin was a little strained. "Yah," he said, his accent deepening as it always did under stress. "Vot you say we go after dem?"

Jim saw then that the side of Lars' face was streaming blood. "You're hit," he said. "Dot is nothing," Lars grinned. "Ven they hit me in the head it does not hort."

"You—" Jim broke off as a bullet snarled past his ear. He cursed, his head snapping around. For that shot had come from the rear!

An instant later one of Gaines' men let out a panic-stricken yell. "They're sneakin' down on us from behind—a slew of them. We ain't got a chance!"

Jim Clane snarled, "If they're comin' that way, turn and fight 'em that way." He got to his feet and ran crouching towards the rear, flinging over his shoulder to Lars, "You hold 'em here."

What the Gaines man had said was true. The canyon above swarmed with Varro men, who boiled out of cover, yelling.

JIM DROPPED his Winchester. The twin guns at his thighs leaped into his hands and began an even deadly roll.

Before the savage accuracy of that fire, the Varro crowd gave back, took cover. But that was only a temporary respite, Jim knew. After a little, the Varro men would think to send gunmen up to the top of the ravine and attack from three directions. Thus it would not be long before Jim and the rest were wiped out.

A bullet took him in the thigh and sent him face downward to the rocks of the canyon floor. Other lead plucked at his shirt as he struggled to pull himself up again. Beside him, the Gaines' man who had yelled was thumbing the six-gun, his face white and strained but set with sudden determination.

Jim grinned at him feebly. "That's the stuff, son," he grunted. "We'll go, but we'll take some with us!"

And then it came.

The great, full-throated fighting yell which was sweeter than any music to Jim Clane's ears. It was Silver Trent's voice shouting *"A nosotros, Los Halcones!* Hell's Hawks, to me!"

The rallying cry of the Hawks! Jim Clane had heard it in a hundred tight spots but it had never put the lift of life in him before as it did now.

Varro's men knew that cry, too. They had gone down to defeat before, and the sound of it put the chill of fear in their bellies.

And behind that first yell came Pablo's voice, lifted in its savage wolf howl; and Magpie's yipping fighting yell. And another, a new voice, shrill and berserk. Behind those shouts came a great drunken exuberant roar.

Jim Clane laughed a little brokenly. Doc Brimstone!

But the guns were hammering now. Jim saw a Varro man dart from cover and meet lead that stopped him dead in his tracks. Another tried to raise his hands in surrender, but he was too late.

It was over. The Varro crowd were panicked by that unexpected slashing attack from the rear. Those who were not shot down surrendered quickly.

Behind Jim, Lars Johanssen's bellowed defiance had taken on a tone that was at once triumphant and more urgent. In front, Silver appeared like a gaunt ghost with blazing eyes, blood streaked on his face. Behind the others followed, faces darkened by powder smoke, wild with the lust of battle.

As Jim turned, they swept past him, but he crawled fast enough to be in on the final scene of that fight.

The Varro men in the valley had closed in, in a swift desperate attempt to take the rear before Silver and the others could win. They had driven Lars and the others back, and now they hit the mouth of the canyon with a rush.

It turned out to be bad timing, for they were crowded there in the canyon mouth when Silver and the others hit them, guns hammering sudden death, relentless in their savage charge.

Jim saw Lars Johanssen get to his feet, streaming blood like a bull the picadores have worked on, and go berserk. In moments like that, guns were no good to Lars, except as clubs. His huge form waded into the close-packed Varro ranks, hamlike hands wielding the barrels of Colts that seemed like ten-penny nails in his fingers.

Behind him and then beside him, Silver's guns hammered,

fast and deadly, with Magpie on the other side, his ancient hoglegs comparatively slow but very sure.

And Pablo, the Pious, yelling blasphemies and fighting like an enraged saint. Darting in and out, like an infuriated bantam, was a small figure that shot wild with a sixgun in one hand and stabbed like lightning with a knife in the other.

There weren't enough Varro men—there couldn't be enough Varro men!—to stand up against that. They broke and ran, stumbling over their own dead and wounded.

Only one figure preceded them, scuttling faster—a hunched black figure on a great black horse. El Diablo!

Silver stood grim-faced, staring after him, with sudden bitterness in his eyes.

But as he watched, a figure lifted up out of the brush and steadied a Winchester on the black racing figure. It was Square Dollar Gaines.

Silver watched with his heart suddenly in his throat. He saw the rifleman's form tense; saw a slender girl's body flung against him as he fired.... And saw El Diablo ride on unharmed!

After that Square Dollar came to Silver with tears in his eyes. "I'd have had him," he said, shamefacedly, "but the gal stopped me. She said it would be murder—as though you could say murder about a human sidewinder like that!"

Silver looked at him and then at the girl broodingly. "Women are women," he said slowly, "but I'm glad it happened that way. Maybe I'm wrong, but I'd have been the sorriest man in Mexico if you had gotten him then."

"Hell! I haven't done anything but cause you trouble—and I haven't even helped you," Square Dollar said bitterly.

Silver smiled at him, "You've helped us have a good fight," he said. "That's our business. And there's your herd, ready to drive to the Border. I don't think you'll have any more trouble now."

Doc Brimstone hollered at him, suddenly more red in the face than ever. "You will, if you don't lie down an' get attended to now, you idiot!"

Silver looked suddenly tired. "I reckon I can now," he said with difficulty. "Do your best, Doc—" He looked out to the mouth of the valley where El Diablo had disappeared and his eyes were bleak— "I've still got a small job to do."

"Then git on the ground," Doc Brimstone growled, "and let me get at those wounds."

Silver smiled at him again, and then his eyes turned toward Joselito, warming. "First," he said, "I'd like to introduce you to a new member of the Hawks!"

Joselito stared at him with his eyes big. "Me?" he whispered. "Me?"

Then his small figure straightened and a great, overwhelming pride swelled the bantam chest. "But yet will I do something to deserve it," he said with his eyes blazing. "Wait and see!"

"That's talkin', son," Magpie's hand fell on his shoulder. "Glad to have you with us."

A quick, short cheer burst from the other throats and warm hands sought his. Joselito shook his head, still half unbelieving. And then his chest swelled even farther. "Wait until the woman hears of this," he burst out. *"Por Dios,* but she will walk softly then—as a woman should!"

SILVER TRENT'S BLOOD-
BOUNTY FEUD

T HE MEXICAN stepped out onto the dance floor
and caught the señorita by the elbow, whirling her out of
Silver's arms just as the music died away. He spat an epithet at
the girl and slapped her, hard.

The blow almost knocked the girl off her feet; she staggered,
her startled cry tapering off into a gasp.

Silver hit the Mexican as a kind of reflex action, and regretted
it instantly. The blow was square to the button and it was almost
certain that the Mexican did not know what had hit him, even
while he was arching through the air to land on the tips of his
shoulder blades and then roll over silently on his face.

Silver knew it was the wrong thing to do an eighth of a
second after his right hook started, but that was a lot too late.
This fiesta had been wrong to start with. There was something
in the air which whispered loudly that men here were ready for
trouble. And Silver Trent had disregarded that, because—well—
this was relaxation after the dangerous job just finished. And
besides, the Border line from this Texas town was not much
farther than Silver could heave an empty sixgun. There was
safety enough in that.

Only, now, and immediately—even before the real trouble
started—he knew that he had been wrong; a fatigue-dulled fool

Silver's right gun spoke...

who had been dupe of his wish to find fun for himself and his men after a tough job well done.

He saw a silent man in a red and black serape hit Magpie Myers even before he saw the glitter of the knife leap towards his own gizzard. His left hand struck upward in the old defense, and he saw the knife flash past his shoulder as he plunged to the right and down.

Above him, from behind, a machete whipped the empty air

where his neck had been. He caught the ankles of the man with the knife and jerked him from his feet, then swung over on his back, driving his heel at the belly of the machete-wielder. His heel hit flesh as the blade drove for his forehead.

The machete point hit the dust beside him, and its owner went down with an agonized grunt.

Trent, on his back, had a glimpse of the tough face of a lawman—he had already decided that. But the man possessed little of the manner of a lawman now. There was a faint flicker of alert interest in those hard, granite-gray eyes, but there was nothing of the stark triumph a lawman ought to have at the sight of Silver flat on his back with a crowd surging over him.

And that was what was happening. This fiesta crowd was suddenly berserk.

Silver's big, superbly muscled haunches came up under him, pistoned him erect. His arms flailed his fists exploding like cannon on the jaws of the mob that assailed him.

The whole fiesta crowd had concentrated on him. He saw knives flash, guns appear out of gaudy Mexican sashes.

These were glimpses while his fists flailed. He saw Magpie's spidery tough form get up and go down again. Then Ricardo's tense voice ripped out at him. *"Jefe!* Out of here. It is a trap!"

And there was Jim Clane, stocky, redheaded, exploding dynamite, coming toward him like a whirlwind. He saw this in the instant that something hit him in the back of the neck, numbing him, driving him to his knees.

He dove at the shins of the man in front of him and felt the numbing slam of the same blunt thing on his shoulder blade. Then he was struggling up and yelling. "To me, *Los Halcones.* We ride!"

IT HADN'T taken Ricardo's voice to warn him. He was fully conscious now that this was a trap and that the four of them were too badly outnumbered to make a fight of it.

Ricardo swung in at one of his sides and Magpie at the other. But where was Jim Clane?

He turned and saw the whirlpool of bodies that marked Jim's

progress. Then the swirl parted to show him a knife driven into Jim's body.

Silver cursed savagely and plunged back into the crowd. A sixgun crashed; the slug ripped the hat from his head.

Magpie yelled into his ear, "Come on, ye dang fool! It's you they want, an' they're ten to one! Come here!" And Ricardo pleaded, "*Jefe!*"

Silver whipped out his sixguns in a blue blur. Something thin and hot slid between his ribs with so much shocking force that he thought at first it was a forty-five slug. Behind him Magpie cursed and Ricardo snarled, and something hit die ground heavily. There was an explosion in Silver's head and then a lot of explosions, very fast, and the fiesta grounds did a dance. That was all be knew.

When he came to, he was in the saddle, with Ricardo supporting him. After a while he remembered.

"What happened to Jim?" he asked.

There was a silence. He repeated his question, and this time his voice had a burr of menace in it.

Magpie said irritably, "Look, Silver, we couldn't do anythin' for him. We— it was all we could do to git our own hides out of there."

Silver looked at him with bitter contempt. "Your hides!" he thundered.

Their horses' hoofs pulled up a rise and followed a declivity into a narrow canyon.

"All right," Silver admitted reluctantly, "my hide, then. But what happened?"

It was an apology, and both Magpie and Ricardo knew it.

"Damn if I know," Magpie said, relieved and at the same time thoroughly worried. "It looked to me like some kind of a set-up. Why, hell! There was some hombre that slugged me before the thing had hardly started. They was layin' for us—but Gawd only knows why."

Silver frowned. "You think the American hombre that was hanging around had anything to do with it?"

Magpie shrugged. "He smelt like law to me. I was goin' to look him over, when all at once everythin' busted. I didn't have the chance."

"Same here," Silver murmured. He shook his head impatiently. "That hardly gets us anywhere. What we're up against is gettin' Jim Clane back. Was he bad hurt?"

Magpie looked unhappy. "Plenty, is my guess! But hell we had all we could do to drag you out of there. That thing was plenty bad."

Silver's eyes hardened. "It'll be plenty bad for somebody when we get back there."

"You take it easy," Magpie growled. "You're plenty hurt yourself.

"Hurt!" Silver snarled. "Hurt, hell!"

But there was that in him which told him he was hurt. His head ached like hell, and his side was a stab of pain with every step his horse took.

The knife blade had slid between his ribs at an angle, luckily missing lungs and all vital organs, but the wound was deep and he had lost a lot of blood. A shot from behind that had creased his skull deeply had knocked him out. A bad concussion had kept him unconscious for hours. He knew he had to get back to the hideout and the care of Doc Brimstone, his drunken but highly competent physician. But not right away.

"Too far," Silver said. "We'll lay up in the shade durin' most of the day, but come evenin' we ride back. If those hellions haven't killed Jim, we'll bring him back with us. If they have—"

His face hardened and the savage yellow light in his eyes finished the sentence for him.

DAWN FOUND them camped deep in the hills. Magpie cooked bacon, tortillas and coffee over a dry chip fire that gave no smoke—a routine precaution of the hunted; just as it had been routine to pick a camp site with a line of retreat in two directions and some possibility of defense. There was no particular reason to expect attack. It wasn't likely that those hombres who lived on the Texas side would cross the Border after them, having missed their kill as it had been planned. Going after Silver Trent in his own territory was too dangerous. Not to speak of the fact that the trio had covered trail as well as they could in the darkness.

But these men lived with danger as a constant companion. And there was never any way to tell from which direction Rurales or Government troops might jump them. The law in Texas wanted them badly. And certain powerful haciendaros in Mexico, notably one Esteban Varro, called El Diablo, hated them as some men hate the sight of holy water.

They were only able to live at all because there wasn't an unbought common man in all of northern Mexico who did not swear by the name of Silver Trent, or who was unwilling to take almost any risk to help him or any member of his gang.

Silver with his head still hammering and the pain in his side bringing weakness and nausea, had to force himself to eat.

Afterward he stretched out on his blankets, and was dead asleep by the time he had closed his eyes.

When he woke it was mid-afternoon. The shadow had moved away from the greasewood grown bank where he had lain down and the full power of the sun was hammering at him. He was bathed in sweat, but the hammering in his head had subsided. The wound in his side made him wince when he moved, but the stab of pain was nothing to what it had been.

Magpie, lying some yards from him, came awake at his first movement, his faded blue eyes at once sharp and alert. There was no sign of Ricardo until a sound overhead drew Silvers attention. He saw Ricardo grinning at him from the brush up on the high bank.

"How you feel, *Jefe?* Better?"

Silver grinned back. "Why not, amigo? Come on down. We'll cook up a little grub and then git ridin'. You had any sleep?"

"Cieriamente! The old one took the firs' watch."

He came scrambling down. Magpie, wordless, was already building a fire. While he cooked, Ricardo went down to where the canyon widened along their backtrail and saddled the horses.

They had beans and sourdough biscuits and coffee. Silver had just begun drinking when a voice rained, "Take it easy. These things hit where I want 'em to."

THE MAN who had stepped from a jut of the canyon held a

sixgun in each hand as though they had grown there. He had a look about him that meant business. He wasn't more than ten paces away.

The sun was behind the gunman's back, keeping his face in shadow. It was a second before Silver knew who it was. At that second, his racing mind was busy with the simple elements of the situation. Whoever this was, he knew what he was about. It took a good man to get this close without being heard; and it took a smart one to come in with the sun at his back.

These things, together with the plain danger in the whole set of the man's figure, were warning enough for Silver to keep still.

Then he saw who the man was, and his anger grew.

Maybe the newcomer saw the yellow flare of it in Silver's eyes for his gunhands stilled suddenly and just a touch of tension appeared in the easy slouch of his body.

He said curtly, "Get your hands up over your head! You're liable to stay healthier that way."

Silver could hear Magpie swear under his breath and Ricardo's low, almost voiceless snarl, but he kept his eyes on the gunman's face. Slowly he lifted his hands. It was a painful effort to lift them; everything in him protested against it. What he wanted to do was to jump with them until he could get them around this man's throat.

When he spoke he made his voice quiet. "So it's you. I thought you were behind that ruckus last night."

"You're wrong," the gunman snapped, "but that don't mean I didn't know how to turn it to advantage."

The lawman's gun was hammering...

"What happened to Jim Clane?" Silver asked. He could not keep the burr of danger out of his voice.

"Don't git in a sweat," the gunman advised. "You two hombres, edge around until you're on a line with your boss, an' keep them hands high."

"Why, you—" Ricardo choked. For an instant, fear chilled the back of Silver's neck as though a cold breeze had blown on it. He knew Ricardo's temper and knew that the knife in the throwing holster behind his shoulder was temptingly near his raised right hand. Looking at the newcomer's face showed him that this man was not as calm as he seemed. His eyes were a fraction too widely opened, the lids stretched a little. He was keyed to killing.

He made his own voice calm, even indifferent. "Take it easy, boys, and do what the gent says. I got an idee he wants to make palaver."

"Smart," the gunman rasped. "I'm beginnin' to see how you lived this long. Pull your guns out of your holster one at a time, slow, with your thumb and 'forefinger. Toss 'em behind you."

When the three had obeyed, Silver said dryly, "Better take that throwin' knife from behind your right collarbone, Ricardo. The gent evidently hasn't seen that."

CHAPTER 2
GUNS TALK LOUDEST

THE GUNMAN crouched a little, the tension around his mouth suddenly sharp. "Keep your hand away from it," he said crisply.

He edged around until he was behind Ricardo. He drew the knife out, holstering one of his guns to do so.

Ricardo looked at Silver like a child who has been betrayed by an adored parent.

The gunman came around in front again. "That was smart, too," he said to Silver. "See that you don't get too smart."

There was suspicion in his eyes but Silver saw too that some of the man's tension had gone.

He sat down on the opposite side of the fire, still holding a cocked Colt in his hand. "Now we can talk."

"I asked you what happened to Jim Clane," Silver said coldly.

"If you mean your red-headed friend, he'll live—if I want him to. I got him where he's safe."

"And who are you?" Silver studied the man.

The man looked at him, level-eyed. "Daggett," he said grimly. "Hellfire Daggett, Dep'ty Sheriff of Pinon County Arizona."

"What do you want of me?"

"It ain't *of* you—it's *you*. The dodgers in my office add up to $10,000."

Silver stared at him unbelievingly. "An' you came down here figurin' to take be back an' collect?"

"Listen, Trent," Daggett snapped, hard-eyed. "You got a rep that would stretch from here to hell an' back, but don't let it fool you. You're just one more outlaw to me."

Magpie Myers swore. Ricardo snarled law a panther.

Silver cut them short. "What did you want to talk about then? It looks like you got me."

"An' I can take you back—all three of you," Daggett said. "But nobody but a dude fool lugs more baggage than he has to. I've heard two things about you—long enough to almost begin to believe 'em. One is that you keep your word. The other is that you'll do anythin' for one of your own men. Well, I've got one an' he'll hang unless I bust him out of the jail he's in. Give me your word that you'll go back with me, peaceable, an' I'll give you mine that hell go free the minute you're in jail. An' that ain't all. These boys can go free, too. That's the deal I'll make with you. Take it or leave it."

Silver rubbed his nose thoughtfully with his left forefinger, and felt, rather than saw, Magpie observe it.

"You damn bounty hunter," Magpie said. There was no anger in his tone, just contempt. "You wouldn't git ten miles toward the Border with Silver or us either before somebody made skunk-steak out of you. You ain't only a damn carrion-eatin' buzzard; you're a splay-brained fool besides. You come out here with a cock an' bull story about not havin' pulled that try at murder last night an' then you want us to take your word for somethin'. The word of a back-stickin' killer!"

DAGGETT'S FACE whitened with anger. For a moment, Silver was afraid he would shoot Magpie out of hand.

But he snapped, "You're a liar—you bat-eared old crawfish. Mob murder ain't my line. An' if I git any more lip out of you I'll pistol-whip you until they won't know which aide of your head to turn upwards when they bury you."

"That fits in," Magpie drawled. "When I haven't got a gun. I shore wouldn't put it past you."

Daggett turned his gaze on Silver savagely. "You better make him shut up," he snarled.

Silver picked up a twig, began to draw designs with it at the edge of the fire ashes. "I reckon he is a little too close to the line," he murmured.

Magpie laughed nastily. "You see that strip of bacon lyin' there," he said to Daggett, "I want to show you somethin'."

He stretched out sideways, almost falling over, as he reached for the bacon. The movement was not sudden, but also it was

105

not slow enough. Daggett's gun muzzle swung towards him. "Keep still, you—"

Everything happened at once then. Silver's hand flicked out like a lizard's tongue and swept the coffee pot into Daggett's face. Daggett yelled as the scalding liquid splashed him. His gun blasted wild. Silver flung himself forward, beating Ricardo's catlike pounce by a hair's breadth, his left hand on the gun and his right reaching for the bounty hunter's throat.

In the same instant, without any warning at all, a ragged salvo of gunfire broke out behind him. Lead snarled over his head like a swarm of infuriated hornets.

For a split second he lay rigid, then he twisted the gun out of Daggett's hand, snatched the other from his holster and whirled to face the fire from behind.

Ricardo already had his hands on Daggett, and Silver didn't think the tough lawman would be a match for Ricardo's bob-cat fury.

The fire had come from where the horses had been hobbled. Silver could see smoke drifting up from the brush fifty yards away; he could see a head, sighting over a Winchester barrel.

Silver's right gun spoke. The head jerked back and sank down slowly.

Magpie had completed his attention-grabbing fall and had instantly begun to roll to where his guns lay. Now their voice was added to that of the Colts Silver held.

The staccato roll of the four sixguns, searching the bushes from which a sharp fire still came, covered the vicious sounds of the struggle behind Silver's back. Then there was the sound of a head being beaten against rock and Ricardo's snarl in Spanish: "That should keep you a while, you treacherous dog."

An instant later Ricardo had got his guns, too.

"Get down, you idiot," Silver snapped. He had emptied Daggett's guns, and now he reached for his own.

Ricardo waited to fire another shot, and took a slug in the shoulder. The impact knocked him down.

Silver swore softly, searching for the ambusher who had made this first hit.

A moment later a figure crawled into the field of his vision. It was Daggett, blood dripping from his head. Silver saw him pick up one of Ricardo's guns and instantly trained one of his own guns on the lawman. But Daggett had no eye for Ricardo. He crawled on a few feet, lay down and began to fire methodically into the bushes ahead.

Was he shooting at his own men?

A SUDDEN burst of firing from the rim of the small valley drew Silver's attention. Reinforcements had evidently come up for the other party, and this crowd was above them. The inequalities in the canyon floor which had given them a meager cover against the first attackers were useless against these newcomers.

Silver's gaze snapped to Ricardo, saw that he was recovering from the first shock of his wound.

"Keep down, Ricardo," he called urgently. "Crawl back toward the horses. We got to get out of here."

Obediently, Ricardo began to crawl back. Magpie, Silver saw, was shooting now at the crowd on the rim, spacing his shots carefully, as though he were at target practice. Daggett, evidently hadn't yet noticed the newcomers.

Silver crowded shells into his empty guns. "Get back, Magpie. We're goin' out." Magpie nodded and began to slide backward, while Silver's guns hammered first at the rim crowd then at the others. Between shots he saw one of the men on the ridge stand up, turn completely around and then dive headfirst into the canyon. Silver's glance met Daggett's.

"That's one of the sidewinders, anyway," Daggett said.

"Get back, we're goin' out," Silver told him.

Daggett nodded and began to inch back, stopping to fire again every foot or so.

It was as much luck as good shooting that kept any of them from being seriously hit as they backed around the jut of the canyon.

After that, they got to their feet and ran, with Silver lifting Ricardo along with them. The canyon outcropping protected them from the view of their attackers for the first twenty-five yards, but beyond that they had some fifty yards of open canyon to cover.

It was Daggett who saved them from that run under fire.

"Up! Up here!" he ripped out.

Silver saw that there was a crude stairway of rock that led up to the rim of the canyon. Half carrying Ricardo, he went up, the others following. For a second they were exposed at the top, then high brush covered them.

Silver followed the rim of the canyon until he reached the first bend, then went to the edge to look down. As he had expected, their horses, which had stampeded at the first volley, were there, trying to forage some nourishment from the greasewood and catclaw that grew sparsely along the canyon floor.

They went down fast and got into the saddle. Silver tried to help Ricardo up, but Ricardo had recovered enough to refuse furiously. It was plain that he was violently ashamed of having been knocked out by a slug in the shoulder.

When they were both mounted, Silver saw that Daggett was in the saddle of Magpie's horse, with Magpie up behind him. And Ricardo's guns—the ones Daggett had been using—were stuffed into Magpie's belt, while one of Magpie's guns was centered in the lawman's back.

"I thought we better bring this sidewinder along with us," Magpie said. "He seems to like to talk. Mebbe he'll do some talkin' that's more interestin' than before."

IT LOOKED as though the tables were turned. But when they had ridden fast and far enough to risk making camp again, there began to be a doubt of that. Daggett stubbornly refused to tell where Jim Clane was.

Ricardo, pale-faced from his wound went paler still with fury. "Let me have him a little while, Silver," he begged. "I promise that he will talk then."

Silver shook his head.

Magpie cut in grimly. "I ain't much on Apache ways in gineral, but this rattler, has his tangs sunk into Jim, an' I've knowed times when bein' staked out on an ant hill set a gent's tongue waggin' so's you could hardly stop it."

Daggett's face lost color, but his expression remained stubborn.

"Better call off your wolves," he rasped at Silver. "I've already told you once that this Clane is goin' to hang if I ain't back by noon tomorrer. I ain't such a fool as to make this play unless I could back it up. Puttin' me on no ant-bill ain't goin' to make me talk. If you or Clane. Them are my cards an' I'm standin' pat on em."

Silver continued to watch him thoughtfully. He was beginning to have a hunch that Daggett meant what he said. Bounty hunter or not, there was a courage and directness in the man that added up to a kind of tough honesty. Silver remembered that Daggett's eyes were clear when he had triggered that last time and dropped one of the attackers that Silver had thought were Daggett's own men. However, it could have been a ruthless, quick-thinking trick, to save his own skin.

Ricardo said again, his eyes hating Daggett, "Let me have him, *Jefe*. I know you have never put any hombre to the torture. But what does this dog deserve? He tried to have you murdered, in the back, last night. And now he has Jeem. He says it is Jeem's life or yours. But I say it is Jeem's life or his—and I know which one to choose. A man would have to be an imbecile to believe this animal, or to make a bargain with him."

"Ricardo's right," Magpie snapped.

Silver shook his head again. "Mebbe not," he said. He was well aware of what this choice would mean if he were taken north of the Border, under arrest. They wouldn't be careless with him. He wouldn't be left in any small jail. He'd be taken to Tucson or Santa Fe, or San Antone. Maybe even to Dallas, and every precaution would be taken to see that he was kept safe until he could be hanged. If he agreed to what Daggett suggested, the chances of his not stretching rope would be one in a thousand.

On the other hand, there was Jim.

Unless Daggett was lying....

Silver came to one of his characteristically abrupt decisions. "Here's the deal I'll make with you," he said curtly. "You deliver Jim to me, alive and not so bad hurt that he's goin' to die anyway, and I'll let you take me, guaranteein' that you ain't interfered with by any of my men until I'm safe in any jail you pick. What you say about me gain' to jail before you deliver Jim, don't go."

Daggett's eyes had a sudden gleam in them, but he hesitated.

"It's that or the anthill," Silver said evenly. "Take it or leave it."

RICARDO WAS looking at him slack-jawed. Magpie burst into furious and profane protests.

Daggett still hesitated, his eyes shrewd.

Silver eyed him, poker-faced. He had guessed that Daggett had seen a man who had been given the anthill treatment, and that horror was never to be forgotten.

Daggett's eyes narrowed. "We meet where I say, then," he said. "Just you and me an' these two. Your pardners here ride off with Clane an' you ride off with me. A deal?"

"Yes."

"You're guaranteein' to handle these hombres, so they don't try to pull anythin' after Clane's in their hands?"

111

"It won't be needed. They know that even if they killed you, I'd ride in and give myself up, havin' passed my gord."

Daggett got to his feet, in his eyes. Silver could see the strain the man had been under. Yet he had not shown it when it might have weakened his hand.

"I'll be goin' now," the lawman said. "Meet me tomorrer night on the main road leadin' south into the town of Las Pumas. There's a stone bridge over an arroyo about a mile out of town. I'll be there with Clane, two hours after sundown." He turned and moved toward his horse.

Magpie swore bitterly. "Had him in Mexico all the time! Silver, damn it, you sold yourself out for nothin'! We could have made him talk an' busted Jim out of that hoosegow as easy as liftin' the first drink after a dry ride!"

Ricardo spat contemptuously. "Are you beliving it? Jeem ees nowhere near Las Puntas. Maybe he ees not even alive. This bounty grabber will set a trap. Why do you theenk he made certain that only we would be there? *Tres hombres*—free! To ride up at night to a breedge where will be twenty, feefty men hiding. *Dios*, Seelver! I would not have believe this of you!"

Silver drew a slow breath. There was a sudden bleakness within him, a heaviness. There was too much chance that Ricardo might be right.

The blazing ball of the sun dropped behind the western rocks as though somebody had cut the string by which it was being slowly lowered. Dusk drifted into the harsh rifts in the badlands like a blue mist.

"I'll take first watch," Silver said wearily. "Any grub left, Magpie?"

"Why keep watch?" Magpie asked bitterly. "Ricardo's right. That sidewinder's got his booby trap set now. His boughten killers won't take the trouble to start anythin' more before tomorrer night."

Silver moved toward the box canyon mouth. "We'll keep watch, anyhow," he said, "on the off chance that Daggett was tellin' the truth."

CHAPTER 3
RENDEZVOUS WITH DEATH

IT WAS a gloomy trio that hit the trail next day for the rendezvous with Daggett. Ricardo's face was pale, except for the sharp flush of fever high on his cheekbones, and he rode in a sweat of pain.

Silver was in better shape. The hammering in his head had subsided, having nothing but a soreness, and after an hour the wound in his ride warmed to the movement of ruling, so that the pain was less. Worse than pain was the growing sense of doubt and uncertainty about Daggett.

Silver had tried to persuade Magpie and Ricardo to stay behind, but that, of course, had been useless. He could feel his confidence and optimism leaking out of him like the blood from his wound.

Dusk showed them the lights of a town ahead.

"Kind of early, ain't we?" Magpie said. It sounded surly, as all of his few remarks on that ride had sounded.

Silver said nothing. If he had been sure of himself, he'd have smiled at Magpie's mood. But any hint of criticism rapped on the raw nerve of his uncertainty, brought a quick temper up in him.

Ricardo spoke for the first time since he had left camp. "Here's the bridge." The words seemed to be wrenched out of his tight lips, and when he pulled his horse up he slumped a little in the saddle.

Silver looked at him worriedly.

"I want you and Magpie to hole up here in the brush," he said casually. "I'm goin' to ride in an' look the town over."

Ricardo straightened. "This is not one of our towns. You know that well, *Jefe.*"

"No, it ain't," Magpie snapped, "but just the same, it's the first idee Silver's had that makes sense. Why stay here in the trap until it's sprung, when we might git some warnin' by lookin' things over before hand?"

Ricardo sounded temperish. "I didn't say anything against that, I'm just saying that Silver must not go in there alone."

"That goes without sayin'," Magpie returned sourly.

Silver looked at them gloomily. This was about the only way any member of his gang ever disobeyed him, but it was a recognized way over which he had no control. If he could think of a good reason for keeping them here....

"Look," he said. "You remember that hombre we saw on the trail this afternoon—the one that slid over the ridge and disappeared before we could get close to him. Well, I didn't say anythin' right then because I didn't want to be puttin' up any scare about somethin' I wasn't sure of. But—did that hombre remind you of anybody,"

Magpie snorted. "Remind me? It was somebody—that durn sidewindin' Yaqui trailer of El Diablo's."

"Well, if you're sure of that," Silver said mildly, "doesn't it mean anything to you? I figure that it was El Diablo's men that jumped us all along. Likely it was a gang he had hired down at the fiesta. Likely, it was more of his crowd that jumped us there in the ravine with Daggett. That means he's liable to be on our trail still. If I'm ridin' into a hostile town, I'd like somebody to cover my backtrail."

Magpie snorted. "Go try to fool your grandmaw," he growled. "You knew that was Varro's Yaqui as well as I did. An' you knowed right then that it was Varro's doin' all along, just like you had suspected it before. But that don't mean that Daggett ain't been bought by this same Diablo. For me, I'm durn sure he is. An' the danger from El Diablo will come right in town. We took it easy ridin' here, account of Ricardo's wound. You can be damn sure that word has gone ahead of us—from Daggett in the first place, and from the Yaqui in the second. The first thing you're goin' to run into in that town is a bunch of Varro's hired killers, if not Varro himself."

SILVER SHRUGGED. "Come on then," he said. "But we got to make this good. Three is easier spotted than one."

Ricardo said nothing, merely moved his horse ahead. Silver eyed him covertly. He wondered just how far gone Ricardo was.

115

Had he kept silent because he was afraid his voice would betray him? If Ricardo gave out on him in town.… .

It was a chance to be taken.

He kept the pace to a walk, his eyes searching the darkness ahead. The light from the town was a help. Anybody moving ahead would be silhouetted; while the three would be in pretty deep darkness against the background of the hills.

It was luck that the road was deep in dust. It muffled the sound of their horses' hoofs so much that the faint squeak of worn saddle leather was actually louder.

But nothing showed ahead of them. Even when they were exactly on the edge of town, the dim light from adobe doorways showed nothing more alarming than poor Mexicans and their wives lounging before their houses.

Silver led a twisting way, keeping to the darker streets and alleys until they were near the central plaza. He pulled up at the rear of a building whose smell announced it as a cantina. The alley broadened here to give place for a shed before which was an empty hitching rack. It was as good a place as any to leave the horses.

For a moment Silver considered going into the cantina. He knew that Ricardo could stand a couple of stiff drinks, but it was too risky; better take a look at the plaza first. He led the way down the alley to a narrow break between the buildings.

The dark and narrow passage led to the square itself. It gave them a place of vantage from which they could look out from shadow onto the life of the town.

Silver stood there for long minutes, frowning, puzzled. There

116

was nothing, absolutely nothing, which could be called suspicious. No air tension; no hard-looking characters. Nothing, in fact, but the normal life of a Mexican town, awakening now because it was dark, cheerful, lazy and unconcerned. In five minutes of watching, he failed to see anybody who showed that vague, intangible something which marks the stranger in a town.

He began to feel silly.

He had ridden in here with his backbone prickling and his trouble sense singing warnings. And that trouble sense of his was usually pretty reliable. It was a definite thing in him, to be trusted as much, he had learned, as his sense of sight or touch. In fact most of the times he had gotten into bad trouble could be traced to his having disregarded its warnings. If he had listened to it at that fiesta, for example, this Jim Clane affair never would have occurred.

A couple of barefooted peons saw the three in the alleyway and looked startled. Automatically, their pace increased a little and they craned their heads to look back as they walked on.

Silver knew that lie had better do one thing or the other—fade out of town or else come out into the plaza and stroll as innocently as everybody else.

"Come on," he murmured to the others. He stepped out into the open.

His sense of trouble hadn't subsided, but there certainly was nothing for it to feed on. The sight of them, even with Silver's bandaged head and Ricardo's arm in its sling, aroused no more than vaguely curious glances.

Silver wondered uncomfortably if he were becoming an old

117

woman. He led the way toward the nearest cantina. At least Ricardo could have his drinks now. Silver felt like he could do with one himself.

HE SLAPPED back the swinging doors of the cantina and went in, stepping sideways automatically, so as to clear the door behind rum. A figure at the bar swung toward him, jaw jutting, eyes flaring angrily. It was Hell-fire Daggett, wearing his deputy's badge openly now, his hands on the butts of his guns.

"Nothin" to drag iron about, Daggett," Silver said quickly.

"No?" the lawman snapped. "What is this anyway? Tryin' to pull a double cross?"

His hands staved on his guns.

"If it was," Magpie said contemptuously, "you couldn't do nothin' about it. Any one of us could give you that much start and shoot you four times before you could clear leather."

Daggett's eyes narrowed. "That's what you think," he said softly. "By God, you talk too much, old windbag. When I've finished this job I'm goin' to come back an' give you a chance to show how fast you are."

"Why not now?" Magpie taunted him.

But Silver cut in. "That'll be enough of that. We aren't tryin' to cross you, Daggett. We come in to see that you didn't try to cross us. You deliver the goods and there won't be any trouble."

The suspicion in the bounty hunter's hard eyes remained.

"I'll be wantin' to see that," he growled. "I been thinkin' ever since I left you that I made a fool deal, trustin' you to bring your pet rattlers along."

Silver laughed without mirth. "I been wonderin' about you

118

some, also. But seein' as we're both in it, there isn't much to do, now but go through with it. Meanwhile, we'll have a drink, until the time comes."

He walked up to the bar and the others followed.

Ricardo staggered a little crossing the room, but caught himself together quickly. *"Tequila,"* he ordered curtly. *"Una doble."*

"I'll take a double one myself," Silver said easily. "What's your pleasure, Daggett."

"Same," the lawman growled reluctantly.

The pockmarked bartender served them with fawning eagerness. He had gone pale at the first promise of gunplay and now his relief and bewilderment at the sudden change in the atmosphere was plainly evident.

Silver grinned. "I reckon he's confirmed now in a belief that all gringos are loco," he remarked. "Here's mud in your eye."

But his mind had sobered instantly. The mere fact that the tension in this room had subsided was a reminder that his sense of trouble was ringing warning bells as strongly as ever.

He thought moodily that this would be the last time he took a chance like this without more of his gang behind him. It had seemed sound judgment to leave the others behind when he started with the herd he had driven across the Border.

Esteban Varro had acquired a new hacienda a hundred miles to the south—a ranch that would run nearly ten thousand cattle and was easily raided. It had seemed a sound plan to send the others to raid that hacienda while he and Magpie and Ricardo and Jim Clane had driven a comparatively small haul across into the States.

It would keep Varro off his trail because he'd be too busy dealing with trouble the gang would be making at the ranch. What he hadn't counted on, he realized gloomily, was the fact that Varro would pretty nearly sacrifice every cow he had for a chance to get Silver Trent. The man's hatred for the outlaw who flaunted him and thwarted him at every turn knew no limits.

And because he hadn't counted on this, he had got himself and the others into a bad spot. He didn't have any doubt at all now that the men who had jumped him twice were Varro hirelings; and be had still less doubt that they wen not too far behind, either, if he knew anything about the abilities of that copper-skinned Yaqui tracker.

The sensation along his spine became suddenly so acute that he was on the verge of pulling out fast, after only one drink.

Daggett's voice checked the impulse.

"Now that you're here," he said, eyeing Silver narrowly, "mebbe we can get goin' with what we got to do, instead of waitin' until the time I said."

"The sooner the better," Silver agreed quickly. "Let's go."

"It'll be you an' me that'll go," Daggett said grimly. "The others stay here. Clane can walk here by himself, while you an' me go our way."

"Have it that way then," Silver said evenly. "But make this fast."

Daggett slid a gun swiftly out of its holster. "You go ahead of me," he snapped. "The hammer of this hawgleg is cocked and the trigger is filed. The muzzle'll be right in your back. If your friends get any quick idees a forty-five slug will bust your backbone even if I'm bit too. Git goin' toward the back door."

CHAPTER 4
THE LAW OF SILVER TRENT

SILVER SMILED faintly and moved off. The bartender was staring at them goggle-eyed. Magpie's face was purple with fury.

"You damn bounty hunter!" he snarled. "When Silver Trent gives his word, it's good. By God, I'll hunt you down for this."

"And I!" Ricardo said, sudden murder in his eye.

Silver said, "Take it easy, amigos. Good luck until we meet again. "

"Which is liable to be in hell," Daggett said hoarsely.

As Silver disappeared through the door Magpie achieved coherence enough to call out: "We'll get you out, Silver—if we have to rip open every jail north of the Border!"

But Silver knew, with a sudden coldness in the pit of his stomach that that was easier said than done.

"What's the program now?" he asked Daggett outside.

"The jail's down there a piece," Daggett said, motioning, "and there's a couple of the boys that'll play dead and let themselves be tied up when I give the word. I fixed that before I got Clane committed." He was talking as they moved, his gun still in Silver's back. "Followin' this alley will take us—"

A forty-five exploded twice in the square in front of the

cantina. Instantly, muffled gunfire answered from within the cantina.

Silver had whirled at the first shot, regardless of the gun in his back. As he turned, he saw half a dozen dark figures race into the alleyway. Four of them darted into the back door of the cantina, guns in their hands. The other two took up positions watching the doorway.

Silver cursed, and his hands slapped at the butts of his Colts. Daggett's gun jabbed him in the ribs. "No, you don't!" the lawman snarled.

"They're after my men," Silver snapped at him.

"You ain't goin' nowhere but with me.

Silver whirled like a striking snake, his elbow hitting Daggett's Colt. The gun exploded, it's slug creasing Silver's ribs like the application of a white-hot iron. His fist snapped to Daggett's jaw, his full weight behind it. The lawman buckled at the knees and went down in a limp heap.

Silver did not wait to see him fall. His guns whipped out, blasted.

The dark figure in the alley nearest him plunged clear across the alley, the top of his head smacking the bottom of the cantina wall. The other gunman yelled, startled, and whirled toward Silver, then put a hand to his stomach and crumpled. Silver did not wait to see that either. He was running toward the back door of the cantina.

Inside, the hammer of gunfire rose to a sudden crescendo. In the cantina kitchen, a gunman turned as Silver plunged in.

The expression on the man's face had no time to change before Silver's gun-barrel slapped him down.

Another man crouched in the doorway, who had been firing into the main room of the cantina, whirled at the sound of cracking bone. Silver shot and knocked the fellow's body aside before it had a chance to fall.

His headlong rush brought him over the body of another dead man into the big cantina room. For a moment, he could see no one but the figure of a Mexican gunman half in and half out of the doorway.

The room was thick with the acrid fumes of powdersmoke.

Kerosene from a smashed lantern burned bluely on the earthen floor.

Then he saw Magpie crouched by the stairway that led to the upper story, and in the same instant a gun blasted from the window at the side, its slug whistling close by his head. Magpie and he both shot at the window in the same instant. Two heads came up over the angle of the bar; guns were raised.

Silver flicked his Colt muzzles that way and shot first, the reports of his own guns blending with the fast wild shots of the others.

"This way, Silver," Magpie yelled. "Up the stairs!"

THEY MADE it, covering each other in turn, with Ricardo's gun already hammering from the balcony above.

The upper rooms, three of them, opened directly off the balcony. They were without doors, had only cotton curtains for privacy.

Silver snapped, "Come on," and plunged through one of the doorways. "I think the back may be clear."

But the instant his head showed, a shot hammered out from below, slapping into the ceiling with a banshee wail. Three other shots slammed through just as he jerked his head back.

"That alley fills up fast," he told the others grimly. "I just cleaned it out a minute ago."

Magpie was at the doorway leading to the balcony. He shot once now, and then again, and cursed.

Silver stood for a moment in the middle of the room, a sudden sick heaviness holding him motionless. He had bungled it This was a trap. There wasn't a chance in a hundred for them to get out. He had bungled everything from the beginning. Jim Clane was lost now, and he had sacrificed Magpie and Ricardo with him.

Magpie said, calmly, "Three more of 'em behind the bar. I'm goin' to try to get 'em." He edged out the doorway.

Silver shook himself impatiently, and walked grim-jawed to the doorway. Ricardo had disappeared—gone to the middle room, likely. No need for instructions now. The others knew as well as he that it was a case of selling out as dearly as possible—unless the bunch below turned yellow. And they showed no signs of that

Lead smashed at him from above the cantina doorway, from outside. He angled a shot through the swinging doors but heard no yelp of pain.

In the same instant, a man jumped up behind the bar with a lamp in his hand, hurled it, and ducked down again. The lamp hit the bottom of the wooden staircase, smashing and spattering kerosene which immediately ignited.

That finished it, Silver knew. The staircase was flimsy wood and dry as tinder. It caught, blazed up.

Silver turned, caught up a blanket from a cot in the room and ran to the stairway. A smash of gunfire greeted him. Lead burnt his arm and a slug creased his head. The blow stunned him, knocked him off his feet. Bullets slammed into the balcony beside him. Magpie was walking toward him on the balcony, his guns hammering a staccato hell-song as he walked. Trust Magpie not to quit shooting. A fool would have run directly to Silver, having the enemy to shoot at will.

Silver got himself together, crawled, then lunged through the doorway. The staircase was really burning now, the flames leaping roaring toward the balcony.

Ricardo staggered out of the center room and backed in with Silver and Magpie. And Silver knew that Ricardo wanted to die with his friends.

He said in a voice that choked a little with the bitterness of his failure: "No point in bein' burned like rats in a trap. Let's take the window—if we go through fast, one of us might get away."

Magpie held out his hand. "Just in case," he said quietly.

The choking in Silver's throat was no longer bitterness. He grasped the old-timer's gnarled paw. Then he turned to Ricardo. *"Adios, Jefe,"* Ricardo said softly. "I think it is better this way than sending you to go alone."

Words wouldn't come. The apology he wanted to make would

have been a kind of insult to such men as these, anyway. He loosened his grip on Ricardo's hand and turned toward the window.

Before he got there a sudden fusilade of gunfire broke out in the, alley below. For a split instant he did not realize that no bullets were coming through the window.

There were yells and curses mingled with the gunfire. Then a harsh, familiar voice called, "By the window, Trent!"

"Daggett!" The exclamation burst from Silver's lips as he jumped for the window.

His first glimpse of the scene showed the lawman down there, his gun hammering. The Varro men, caught by surprise had started to back up, those of them that could after Daggett's first deadly burst of fire. But now, seeing that it was only one man, they stood fast, shooting back. Silver got his guns into action, swiftly, yet deliberately enough to make his aim deadly. Beside him, Magpie's guns began to chant.

Men below reeled and went down. Then there was a sudden almost concerted race for safety.

"Come on!" Silver vaulted through the window. This had to be East, before the ones in front woke up and closed in for the death.

He hit the ground with a jar that ran clear up his backbone and pitched forward, a violent pain in one ankle. Instantly though, he was on his feet again. The alley was momentarily clear. Somebody landed next to him with a gasp of pain and he saw that it was Ricardo who had been lowered as far as possible by Magpie. Then Magpie himself was hanging by his hands from the window sill and dropping. He got to his feet as Silver pulled Ricardo up.

"Old bones," Magpie gasped, grinning, "but they can take it."

A Varro gun hammered up the alley. Silver shot it the flashes. Then they were running to where their horses stomped and snorted nervously in the shelter of the shed.

A moment later something like a cyclone split by streaks of lightning whirled down that street, and Esteban Varro had missed his pounce again. An ill-advised Varroista showed himself for a shot as the four riders swept pest, and he was the tut to die that night....

SILVER LOOKED at Daggett, riding grim-faced at his side.

"What in hell made you take a chance?" he asked curiously.

For just an instant he thought he could discern a kind of embarrassment in the set of the lawman's face. But then the harsh voice rasped out at him; "Hell! You didn't think I was goin' to let a gang of thievin' gunnies do me out of ten thousand iron men!"

Silver roared with laughter.

They had ridden for a full ten minutes before he had asked that question, and there was no pursuit. He pulled from a run to a trot and then halted altogether. "Well?" he said looking at Daggett.

"That don't go," Magpie cut in grimly. "You had your chance, law-dog. It broke wrong for you an' now it's ended. We're obliged to you for givin' us a hand, but we ain't that obliged. We can bust Jim out of that jail without any help from you."

His guns were covering Daggett, their muzzles rock steady and menacing.

Silver said, "I won't do, Magpie. A deal's a deal. You know that You boys get along. I'll give Jim my horse, when we finally get him out. He'll be able to get back all right. And Daggett can hunt up some land of a nag for a prisoner to ride."

"Jefe!" Ricardo's voice was thick. But Silver would not listen.

He moved off quickly, his jaw locked. This, too, was no time for talk.

Behind him Daggett moved, too, in silence. But after a few yards, the lawman said, "Hey, wait a minute."

Silver pulled up. "Look here—" Daggett's voice was strange, "There is somethin' to what that old windbag said. It wasn't exactly your fault that the deal didn't go through right. You mean you're not tryin' to take advantage of that? You're makin' the deal over again?

Silver shrugged wearily. "It's the same deal, Daggett. You know it, and I know it. What's the sense in beatin' around the bush?"

Daggett eyed him silently during a long moment, then he sighed slowly. "Damn if I don't believe you meant to play it straight all along," he murmured.

"Didn't you?" Silver asked briefly.

"Yeah," the lawman answered thoughtfully, "but the deal was in my favor. I don't mind sayin', though, that if they followed orders, there's a dozen men snaked out by the bridge right now, just in case you tried to change your mind."

Silver laughed shortly. "Don't know as I blame you. Well? Do we ride along?"

Daggett reached up slowly and closed his hand over the badge on his shirt. A sharp movement ripped it loose. He held it in his hand a moment. Then he tossed it into the brush. "Damn the law," he said quickly. "You needin' a good gun-hand?"

Silver drew his breath a little sharply. "I can always use one," he said. "But—maybe I don't quite get it."

"Ten thousand is ten thousand," Daggett said, slowly, "but tonight's taught me that there's something more. My side of the law was all right. I reckon, Daggett said, still talking slowly. "But I never found anybody that would stick by it the way you buzzards stick to each other!"

He shook his head impatiently. "Well, if we ride in the other side of town we can still get Jim Clane out without standin' much chance of running into your playmates back there. Do we ride... Chief?"

Silver put out his hand. "I think I'll be kind of proud to ride with you, Hell-fire," he said. And then he turned to Magpie and Ricardo. "You might as well ride along with us, amigos. Get acquainted with a gent who'll be around from now on."

He and Daggett rode on.

Magpie looked at Ricardo whose sudden grin was pale in the starlight "Well, I will be damned!" he said slowly.

Ricardo's grin widened. "Me, too."

Magpie's lips tightened. "And to think I don't ever git a chance to draw on that blowhard," he grumbled.

"Perhaps this ees just as well," Ricardo observed. "He is fast, that one, like greasy lightneeng."

Magpie snorted. But a moment afterwards he began to grin, too.

SILVER TRENT RIDES ALONE

PABLO'S GUN-HAND flicked like a striking copper-head, without warning.

Silver Trent checked the coffee cup before his lips long enough to murmur, "Easy, old one," and then drank.

The man who had come up toward the fire had frozen at the view of Pablo's gun-muzzle. Now, hearing what Silver said, he relaxed tentatively, though his face showed queerly white in the ruddy fire-glow and the flickering light revealed beads of sweat on his upper lip.

Pablo snarled, "Take off your hat, double-crosser!"

The man took off his hat hastily.

Silver looked at him with eyes that held a wicked amusement, putting down the coffee cup and reaching into his pocket for the sack of tobacco and corn-husk papers.

The man before him ran a dry league over dry lips, then he opened his mouth to speak.

"Shot your mout'," Pablo snarled at him, "When *El Jefe* talks to you, then you answer."

The man shut his mouth, and the iridescent beads of sweat were visible on his forehead, now that his hat was off.

Silver Trent laughed a little, silently. "Well, Fenner?" He asked, licking the rolled cigarette. "What's on your mind?"

Slug Fenner swallowed, his eyes running hastily from face to face about the fire and then rushing back to Silver's as though stampeding there for some kind of protection.

"Look, Silver," he said hastily, "I know what I done an' what you must think of me. I—I don't understand it myself. Nothin' like that ever come over me before turnin' yeller, I mean. Hell! I owed you everythin'. I was one of the gang—"

Pablo growled in his throat like a suddenly affronted cata-mount and shoved his gun back into its holster. For the split fraction of a second, Fenner's startled eyes looked relieved, then they froze again as the glittering blade of the knife flowed into Pablo's hand.

"You were not ever of this gang," the Mexican said softly. "Remember that, *hijo del perro grande*. Remember that, and never say again that you were."

Fenner flushed, his jaw jutting out suddenly. "All right," he

Silver raced toward the head, his sixgun hammering...

snapped. "Have it your way." His eyes turned to Trent, "But you know what I mean, Silver." His voice had a hint of appeal in it, but a sudden new defiance was in it also.

Trent looked at him thoughtfully.

This man was one of Silver Trent's two failures. From time to time, Fate threw some new bit of human flotsam into his reach and, rarely, the man turned out to be worth having. When that was so, Trent offered him a chance to run with his famous Hawks. The man who refused that offer was rare. But the man who accepted and then betrayed it was rarer still.

Of the latter there had been one Grulla Ferguson and now—this one.

Trent's hard eyes ran over the face before him, trying to search out the concealed weakness that bad made his initial judgment wrong. It wasn't, at first glance, either a bad face or weak one, despite the natural nervousness that strained it now. The eyes were a trifle too close-set against the strong jut of the nose, but then one of the bravest and most loyal men Trent had ever known had had eyes even closer set than that. The mouth was firm, handsome—maybe a little too handsome?—and the jaw was strong.

"Sit down, Slug," he said evenly.

Fenner sat down a little too quickly, as though his knees had not been too steady, and looked relieved.

"I take it you didn't come back to try to join up again," Trent observed, his voice dry.

Jim Clane, who had brought him, said impatiently, "Look, Silver—why palaver? Ricardo damn near died because of this skunk. Let's take him out an' string him up and get it over for him."

Lars Johansson grunted. "Ya! Dat's right, Chief. I am not killer, like you know. But I tak' d'is neck in my han—an' after, I sleep gude."

Ricardo cut in quickly. "It is not for me," he said quietly in Spanish. "What he did to me is nothing—*denada.* But for all of us, I think he knows perhaps too much. And besides, in the future, men should know that one does not quit *Los Halcones*—nor betray them...."

Silver's eyes narrowed and he said, drily, "It's a point, but then.... What was on your mind, Fenner?"

Fenner caught his breath a little sharply, started to speak and then tautened. It was as if a sudden idea of his own had forced him against his will to speak.

"Listen," he said, his eyes hard, unyielding. "If any of these hard boys think they want trouble with me, they can have it. I joined up in good faith, an' I ain't sitting around takin' everything any gent thinks he wants to deal out."

Jim Clane's eyes lighted up, and automatically his hands went to his guns. "That's me," he snarled. "I want trouble with you, you crawlin' skunk. Plenty of it!"

Silver cut off Jim's growl with a raised hand. "We won't get anywhere this way," he said. "Go ahead, Fenner; say your piece."

"All right," Fenner said, a little breathlessly. "I got somethin' that's good for me an' that's good for you. See? I don't say I did right when I was with you, an' at the same time, I don't say that I ever discovered any reason to believe this Robin Hood business that folks talk about you. I'm figurin' that you're lookin' out for your own end, same as anybody else. An' I got somethin' for your end—anywhere's from twenty to thirty thousand dollars, *oro*—gold." You interested, or do I take my crack at these buckaroos of your'n that think they're so good with their guns, an' then take my leave?"

Silver said, "You've talked a lot of words. What have you really got to tell?"

"Two to three thousand head of rustled cows," Fenner snapped. "You'rn for the takin'!"

HE LEANED forward tensely. "Now listen. When I funked out with you here, I knowed it wasn't no use to come back an' try to explain it so, I sloped an' I ended up in a Texas town, name of Ocotilla. There's a hombre there that's beginnin' to run the place an' he offers me a job as marshal, helpin' him. I'm broke, so I take it.

"My boss—name's Corbin, J.G. Corbin—is figgerin' to take over the town an' the range. The town ain't run right an' the range is broke up amongst a lot of two-bit ranchers and homesteaders that are liable any minute to start ploughin' up the sod an' runnin' good cattle graze. You know how it is with the little fellers they can't make a livin' on cattle alone, an' they aim to do it however they can, an' to hell with what comes afterwards. So what Corbin's doin' is all right with me.

He paused and stared earnestly at Silver. "Only," he said with emphasis, "there's one other pretty big rancher there. Name of Kilvane who owns the K&K brand. He's all right. An', well-well, I aim to marry his daughter Anne, Get it? I got to keep Corbin from ruinin' him. They're fightin' now over water, an' that means life or death to Kilvane. If I had a crowd up there that'd bluff Corbin off—make him know he couldn't tackle the K&K without gettin' the worst of it—why, that wouldn't do me any harm with Anne, or with old Rusty Kilvane. See? An' I could still get along with J.G. Corbin. Get it?"

"I think I catch it," Silver said thoughtfully. "You just want to show this Corbin that you can call up plenty of strength any time you want to. That'll make your hand about strong enough to play it even between Kilvane an' Corbin. An' you'll be hog-tyin' the gal an' the K&K by the same maneuver."

Fenner pulled in a deep breath and let it out softly. "You got it," he said.

"But then, what'll happen when we pull out?"

"They won't know you can't be called back. In fact, they'll figure that if I did it once, why not again? That's what I'll play on. Rather than take the chance, J.G.'ll play along with me."

"Besides, in the meantime," Silver observed shrewdly, "you can begin buildin' up a crew of gun-fighters of your own.

"You got it."

Silver laughed shortly. "All right for you," he said, hard-eyed. "But where do we come in? You already said that we weren't any Robin Hoods—an' you sure were right. I don't mind helpin' out a poor hombre when he needs it, especially if we can make a little profit out of it for our trouble. It's good business. It makes us friends, hideouts, gets us information we need. But this is different. It's out of our territory. What do we get out of it, feller?"

Fenner leaned forward with his jaw jutting and something

like triumph in his eyes. "Corbin's been rustlin' cattle," he said softly, "to break the little guys, one by one. He's been goin' at it strong, an' hasn't tried to market a single head of that stolen beef. It's all been run up into the hills for brand blottin', an' it'll be held there in the best hideout you ever saw until he gets ready to claim it or sell it. There's two to three thousand head of it not far from the Border. An'—I—know—where—it—is!"

Silver's lower lip jutted. "You mean that's our cut," he said grimly, "How much of this beef is guarded?"

"Hell," Fenner said contemptuously.

"He don't keep only three men up there. You can take it without gettin' sweat on a horse."

"An' what'll Corbin think of you for that?"

Fenner grunted. "He'll think he don't want you back again, is all. An' he'll think he better play square with me, an' not monkey around."

Trent pushed his sombrero back with a quick restless hand, so that the firelight showed on the one lick of white hair which ran back from his forehead and had given him the name Silver. His white teeth showed in an even grin.

"Might be a deal," he said with sudden cheerfulness, "if it's like you tell it. How about this Kilvane—he as crooked as you an' Corbin?"

Fenner spat contemptuously. "He's so dumb he'll play it straight, even when it's cuttin' his own throat!"

"An' the gal? Same weakness?"

Fenner looked complacent. "Leave her to me," he said. "I'll take care of her."

Trent nodded. "All right. Get on back. We'll ride on in, gettin' there in a couple of days to look things over. It sounds like it might be worth tryin'."

FENNER STOOD up with his eyes blazing with triumph. "You won't regret it," he said jubilantly. "It'll be one of the best couple of day's work you ever did!"

He stood up and swept his eyes arrogantly around the circle. "If the rest of you birds had as much brains as Silver," he announced, "you'd get farther. Before you get through spending your cut of thirty thousand dollars, you won't be so sorry you had me in the gang once."

Pablo's breath came suddenly short and fast. *"Jefe,"* he begged almost pitifully, "I do not ask much. Let me only cut the throat of this one before he walks off leaving me with a sickness in the belly for ever!"

Silver eyed him coldly. "You had ears to hear what I said," he murmured, hard-jawed. "Did you, then, not hear?"

Pablo subsided with something like a groan.

The others said nothing. Only Ricardo spat, the scornful spurt from his lips sizzling with sudden loudness in the fire."

Slug Fenner laughed and turned on his heel, striding through the darkness toward his horse, *"Aios, hombres,"* he called over his shoulder. *"Hasta la vista."*

Jim Clane's square face purpled until it looked black in the fire light. "Yeah, until we see each other again!" he snarled.

The bitter brightness of his eyes followed the retreating figure through the darkness, then he swung on Silver. "I don't know what's come over you," he raged. "Have we got so that we got to take the beef of a few busted ranchers for our own? Is that the kind of outfit Trent's Hawks have turned out to be? Because if it is—"

Trent's cold voice cut him off, his rocky, homely face suddenly bereft of all friendliness. "I'm not sure what's come over you, Jim. Tryin' to run the outfit now?"

Jim Clane swallowed, his hands sinking almost imperceptibly toward his guns and then relaxed in a gesture of indescribable frustration. Suddenly, he flung away, following Fenner's retreating figure into the darkness.

Trent's eyes followed him with something almost like pity, then returned to the stony-faced circle about the fire. His grin was thin, angry.

"To look at you," he taunted them, "anybody would think we were a lot of priests engaged in profanin' the altar. Did it ever occur to you that we're outlaws—the dodge—with a livin' to make? An' we can't afford to be too particular? Or maybe you better all start in takin' the vows."

Nobody spoke. Only Pablo moved. He whetted his knife on his thumb with sudden violence so that the blood spurted as the keen edge caught and slid in deeply.

"Are we so saintly," Trent asked grinning relentlessly, "that we can't check a crook in his crookedness so we can lift his loot from him—even if you don't happen to like the man that made us the proposition?" His voice hardened. "What shall it be? Your war or mine? Your truth or my truth?"

Nobody said anything. Pablo's face, lean-burning in the fire-light, turned down toward the espurting blood on his thumb.

Ricardo's young, hawklike face showed hooded eyes.

The mesquite root fire crackled and snapped, loud against the utter silence. And overhead the black parchment of the sky showed its immense sidereal illuminations, remote and brilliant and unreadable to mortal eyes—as though its blight page were meant only to throw back to man's ancient affirmations the old, derisive answer: "What is Truth?"

CHAPTER 2
A DRINK WITH C.G. CORBIN

TRUTH FOR Trent, three evenings later, was the main street of Ocotilla with the violent colors in the western sky fading and the dusk coming down. The stores that had already lighted up showed faint pallid yellow streaks across the dust of the road, like bleached spots against the yellow afterglow. And there was that in the air, in the sharp eyes of men, and in the over-quietness and casualness of their gesture, that put a humming along Trent's spine as unmistakable as the first light rasp of catgut across fiddle strings.

But there was nothing tangible to take hold of.

At Silver's side, Magpie Myers' wrinkled face was expressionless, his faded, pale-bright eyes very alert.

"This is wrong, Silver," he murmured out of the side of the mouth.

"Feel it, too, do you?"

Silver's gray eyes wandered with seeming idleness over the street and fixed suddenly on a girl who stood on the porch of

141

the general store. She was slender and lithe as a young willow tree, with dark hair and wide eyes which were fixed on Silver in a kind of startled recognition. He knew that he had never seen her before so her expression could mean only one thing—that she guessed his identity, had known of his coming; in fact, Anne Kilvane.

Just beyond her, at the store's hitch-rack, was a buckboard. An older man with a white mustache and wrinkled eye-corners was stowing packages into the back of it. His head also was turned toward Silver, his eyes keen and questioning.

Beside Silver, Fenner's figure appeared suddenly, as though out of thin air. "The Busted Eagle Saloon," he said, out of the side of his mouth, and passed on. Silver nodded infinitesimally, but his face hardened still more.

The murky gleam of Fenner's marshal's badge disappeared as he gained the boardwalk and disappeared among the strolling crowd of cowpunchers and townsmen.

The Busted Eagle was only a few doors down. Silver and Magpie, with Lars Johanssen a little behind them, pulled up at the hitchrack and dismounted.

A wide-eyed kid of about ten, in jeans that were too big for him and rolled up around the bottom, pulled up in front of them and stared long at Silver's horse.

"Gee," he said softly. "A *palomino!*"

He looked at Silver earnestly. "It is a palomino, ain't it, mister?" He said with his voice trembling a little. "It is, ain't it?"

"Why, yeah, son," Silver said. "It's a palomino, all right."

"Gee," the kid said, awed. "I never seen one before. I seen

some buckskins but I ain't never seen one of them. I—I reckon they ain't many of 'em aroun' these parts. Gee," he said softly, "I reckon you're lucky, mister."

"Well maybe," Silver said. "I got several of 'em. In fact, I got quite a little herd of 'em."

The boy looked at him with a wonder so great that it had a tinge of unbelief in it. "Honest, mister? Gee, there ain't but one other gent that has 'em like that." His eyes took on an unearthly shine. "Silver Trent! He's got a whole remuda of 'em—real ones. That's what they say, anyways, an' I reckon it's true. All perfect—every one of 'em."

His voice rose in an ecstasy of recountal. "The hides of 'em gold as gold, and manes and tails silver as silver. An' not a splotch on 'em, 'cept—'cept mebbe a star on their foreheads, an'—an" mebbe a star the side of their fetlocks. Like—like for wings."

Like a shadow, then, a big man came up out of the alley by the side of the saloon and stood looking on. The sight of him jerked at Silver's attention but did not quite move his eyes. He kept looking at the kid, but in the fringe of his vision he took in the man with something tightening in his stomach.

The man was curiously built, his body giving the impression of cones sunk into one another. His shoulders were wide and his chest was deep, but also his back was deep, so that the whole thing made a section of a sphere. And that section ran down evenly, so that its circumference was equal at the waist and then this waist widened into two equal diminishing cylinders that were the legs.

It was an odd sight, like a man built perfectly out of large, pared, solid sausages.

Silver grinned briefly at the kid and said; "This What's-His-Name's has got some luck, all right. Well, I'll see you, bud." He started to turn away.

"This What's-His-Name?" the kid shrilled at him in sudden outrage. "You mean you ain't hear'n of Silver Trent?"

Trent turned back to him. "I've heard the name," he said, smiling a little. "He's an outlaw."

The kid set his small jaw so that it looked like a young, unripe walnut. "Mebbe he is an outlaw, mister," he said, "but he ain't that kind of a outlaw. He's good. He don't never do nobody no harm unless'n they does what's wrong. Why, Silver Trent—he's the Hawk—*El Halcon de las Sierras!* Why, if anybody does you wrong"—his voice broke high and shrill in excitement—"they'll fix it up—"

He broke off and his small body seemed to shrink as though it had been suddenly deflated. "But I reckon not—any more."

"Why not any more, son?"

"Because they're gonna get him," the kid said dully. "You see, they can, if he ain't lookin' for it. If they can trick him and trap him in. I hear'n 'em talkin'. I hear'n big Jay—"

But the huge cylindrical man stepped forward, clearing his throat.

"Good evening, gentlemen. I see you're newcomers to Ocotilla. I'm glad to welcome you. Corbin's my name. I'm nothin' but just another citizen, but we pride ourselves on our hospitality here."

SILVER SAW now that he had eyes which were oddly round also and queerly colorless. He also saw the kid shrink like a rabbit freezing at the approach of danger.

Silver ignored the newcomer and turned to the kid. "What's your name, bud?"

The kid gasped and his body trembled a little. "Sh-h-ucks, mister. I—wasn't meanin' nothin'. Well… so-long, mister. Mom, she'll be wantin'"—

"Bud!" Trent's voice stopped him as though the snapper of a blacksnake whip had curled round him.

"You ain't afraid, are you? What would Silver Trent think of you?"

The kid stared at him and shivered and then all at once brought himself together. "All right," he said tightly, with his jaw jutted out, "it's him. It's J.G. Corbin. He runs this town— the bully! My mom, she says I got to be nice to that of—that ol' swelled-up bullhead!" He looked at the cylindrical man and burst suddenly into tears. "Now I've done it," he said, "My mom said—" His sobs drowned out the rest of it.

Trent's look at the small huddled figure was gentle and puzzled. Then he laughed a little and went forward.

"Bud," he said softly. "Bud, listen to me. You like palominos?" Trent stared down at him.

The kid's eyes came up suddenly, wondering.

"I only ask you, son," Silver went on, "because I got one that you can have. A colt that's a pure strain, with only a couple of flaws—a star on his forehead and a star on his fetlocks. So I reckon he was born for you, since you'd be the only one that would be romancin' about stars that were wings and wouldn't occur in a thousand years. He's gentle an' already saddle broke. An' he'll be yours now, in just a couple of days."

The kid looked at him, dazed, yet somehow believing. "You— you mean it, mister?"

Silver grinned at him suddenly all out

"Why, yeah, I mean it, bud. You've done me a favor, without maybe knowin' it. An' I try not to forget a favor. You see, son, I'm Silver Trent!"

He didn't stay to watch the breath-caught paralysis of that small figure. He turned to the cylindrical man, caught him by the arm.

"Glad to see you, Corbin," he grinned wickedly, "Come in. Let's have a drink!"

The upper arm underneath his hand was like a reluctant, hardwood log for an instant, then it yielded. Together they walked into the saloon.

THAT ENTRANCE was like the explosion of a small bomb-shell. There was hardly a man in the place who did not stiffen and catch his breath.

Trent's quick hard gray eyes missed none of that. Nor did Magpie's. The oldster said drily, "Silver, I never did know you to work better. But just the same, amigo, not even God knows it *all*."

Silver laughed outright. "What do you think of that, Corbin?" he asked, shaking the big man by the arm. And then his eyes caught those of the bartender.

The bartender was a large and beefy man who had kept

indoors by virtue of his profession. But the pallor he had now could not be blamed wholly on the lack of sunlight. And at this moment his eyes looked like startled raisins in a lump of dough.

"Set 'em up, pardner," Silver grinned at him. "This one's on me."

The bartender stared at him and said, "Y—yessir."

Trent's left hand shot out and grabbed him by the coat-front, yanking him up against the edge of the bar. "And forget about the shotgun," he said softly. "You'd never get a chance to use it."

The bartender put on the pallid semblance of a grin. "Sure— sure," he said faintly, and shot a glance at Corbin, then swallowed and ducked suddenly behind the bar as though looking for glasses.

The room had taken on a deadly silence.

It was broken now by Lars Johanssen's bellowing laughter. "Har! Har!" He roared. "I'm go planty places but now I'm listen to Silver talk to boy like man, an' then talk to man like boy. Tall me," he turned a beaming face on the room, "whan we start fight?"

It had a curious effect. For a moment everybody seemed turned to stone. Even Silver looked momentarily startled, then he laughed too.

"Don't wait, boys. Let's start the party."

His left hand licked up almost carelessly and the knuckles of it took J.G. Corbin just under the lobe of the ear, on the angle of his jaw.

In the far corner the rattler-faced man whipped his hands

to his belt and took Silver's slug in the belly before the Colt muzzles had quite cleared leather.

But that was late, and Silver knew that it was because the man with the ivory guns and the weasel mouth had drawn faster. And he knew in that breath of an instant that he had misjudged, that he had picked the less dangerous of the two men and that very likely he himself was deader than a doorknob. And he wished that Ricardo and Pablo had been a little quicker. All this he thought in the split second before Ricardo's gun blasted from the window and the soft, horrid *thuk* of Pablo's knife sounded in Weasel Mouth's throat.

The lamp Pablo had shot out smashed to the floor with the glass tinkling, and almost instantly the lamp over the bar went out. The crash of it under Magpie's gun showed a sudden eerie blue flare in which the bartender popped up with the shotgun in his hands. Magpie shot him once through the forehead and the blue flare died down as though it had been Hell's special light for that man's death.

Immediately after, the only light in the big room was the light of wildly blasting gun-muzzles.

THE AIR bloomed out darkly, sharp and choking with the acrid fumes of gunpowder. There should have been no sound, 'except the snarling explosions of the Colts and men's deep excited, unwise breathing, or perhaps the panicky scuffle of feet scuttling for safety. But there was another sound, because Lars Johannsen had gone berserk again.

It was a sound of bone smashing against flesh, of skulls cracking together, of fast, gargantuan, pounding feet, of bodies crashing into walls, of the crack of heads against wood, of panicky grunts, wild shots, screams of lead-hit men.

In the darkness those sounds held terror. No man should have been willing to dare random bullet in order to fight with his hands in that pitch-blackness. And the mere fact that someone was doing it, put panic in the atmosphere.

Men gasped, grunted desperately and flung toward the doors. There was the scrape and pound of feet, the gasped curses at the doorways, the sickening smack of gun-barrel through flesh to bone and then Lars Johannsen's barrel-chested bawl, "Who wants some more? Come on, you short-bottomed sons of low-down snakes. I—"

Silver's voice cut the bellow off. "Shut up, Lars. Move out, men. We beat one gun-trap. Let's not bungle into another!"

Silver tumbled out the saloon door, whipped sideways, snapped shots right and left at one imaginary and one real shadow, to cover the exit of his men and them, as they whipped past him, cat-footed swiftly to his horse.

A small figure rose up in front of him. "You—your bridle reins are already over him, Mister Silver," the voice stammered.

Lars and Magpie were lunging to their saddles.

Up-street, a gun blared a crimson and yellow streak in the night, the bullet whining close, splintering a plank of the board walk.

Silver cursed and snarled. "Down! Flat in the dust! And stay there, you bat-eared little fool!"

With the sweep of one hard hand he slapped the kid down into the dirt of the street. Then he swung into the saddle.

Down-street, a Winchester put its thinly wicked crack-across the air. The bullet snicked across Silver's belly, whipping a chunk out of his saddle horn.

Silver waved a hand at the others. "They're up the street, both ways," he said crisply. "Get goin' through the alley. Meet me at the south end of town." Afterward he bent down and snarled savagely, "Keep layin' flat, you dumb-headed, swell little quarter-wit—an' maybe sometime you'll own a palomino of your own!"

He swung his mount and slapped in the spurs. The golden horse jumped a yard straight up and hit the street flattened out like a traveling bullet.

Up-street a crouching figure slammed two fast shots at Silver's animal that drove toward him. It was a figure that Silver had seen and was heading for.

The man tried to run across the street, then changed his mind. He ducked back toward the boardwalk and desperately slammed another shot at Silver as he brought the palomino up rearing. The slug howled past his ear. His right hand whipped out and caught the gunman by the vest and shirt, jerking him up against the horse's heaving flank.

Silver heeled the palomino into the shelter of a space between two buildings as lead mapped around him. His right hand still held the struggling man, dragging him. The excited, stomping horse whipped a hoof down onto one of the captive's dragging feet, and the man cried aloud in agony.

"You double-crossin' son," Silver snarled at him. "You got some reason why I shouldn't put a hot slug through you?"

Fenner whimpered. "I—God, it wa'nt my fault. He got onto me. I swear, Silver, he got onto me an' he forced me into it. He'd of killed me if I hadn't done what be wanted."

"You told him I was comin'."

"He—he'd have tortured and killed me if I hadn't. You don't know him. I didn't know him. I was hopin' for a chance to warn you, but he was watchin'."

"That why you tried to kill me a minute ago, you lyin' skunk?"

"I knowed then it was me or you. Once it went wrong. But only... Oh, only if you'd try to understand, that I never meant—"

"Where are these cows you told me about?"

Slug Fenner pulled a long shaken breath. "Out by the bend of Black Creek," he gasped eagerly. "You follow Horseshoe Canyon, an' then branch left about half a mile before High Wash cuts in. You can't miss that trail—the tracks'll be there all along...."

Trent shook him savagely. "If you've lied to me, I'll boil you in oil. And you can tell your pardner, Corbin, that he can find me at the K&K. Me an' Kilvane are runnin' this range from now on!"

He wheeled the palomino about and sent him plunging across the street into the other alley, and then he was gone.

CHAPTER 3
HELL-BOUND
FOR THE NOOSE!

THE BUCKBOARD was only four miles out when he and his men caught up with it. The rig had pulled

151

up alongside the road before they came up, and when Silver dragged his horse to a rearing halt beside the seat he found himself looking into the muzzles of three guns.

He grinned. "Easy," he said. "You're quick on the draw in these parts."

"Mebbe we have to me," Kilvane told him grimly. "Who are you, and what's on your mind?"

"This," Trent told him swiftly. "Fenner asked me to come here to help you out. And Fenner, with Corbin, tried to double cross me. He missed it. You wasn't in town. Here's what happened."

And he told them the story.

"The point now is," he ended, "that I've sent word to Corbin that he can look for me at your place. I won't be there unless I have to. How many men have you got, and how long can you hold out in case he looks me up there?"

Kilvane sat a long moment in silence while the palomino's dainty hoofs beat a restless tattoo in the soft dust of the road. Then he said drily, "This is a lot of help I didn't ask for."

"And don't need," the other, younger man cut in sharply. He turned up a square-cut hard-jawed face to Silver. "If you're mixed up—even enough to be double-crossed—with Slug Fenner, why, speakin' for me, I can do without you."

Silver looked at him somberly. "Mebbe you're right, friend," he said. "Do you know who I am?"

"Trent, aren't you? Some kind of outlaw."

Silver chuckled. "How'd you know it?"

"A kid told us. I've heard somethin' of you, anyway—not that I believe everythin' I've heard."

"Oh, yes—the kid," Silver said softly. "Who was that kid, anyway?"

The hard voice grated back at him. "Nephew of mine, if you want to know. Name of Duke Benson. Mother owns a small spread hereabouts. Dad's dead. And, mister, I'm lookin' out for him—an' her. Mebbe you mean all right. But don't make any mistakes. Like most kids, this one's a fool for an outlaw, but I'm not. Get it?"

"I get it," Trent said, a little bitterly. "Mebbe you're right. So where do we go from here? You able to take care of Corbin all by yourself?"

The girl hit one clenched fist into the palm of her hand with sudden energy. "No!" she answered and Silver could hear the click of her teeth. "No, he can't!"

The youngster tautened. "Anne," he snapped, "you keep qui—"

"I won't," she cut him off passionately. "Listen, Dan Benson, I told you I'd marry you and I'll go your way, whatever it is and wherever it is. But that doesn't mean that I've got to go with a gag in my mouth. I'll say what I think to the longest day we live!"

She turned on Silver. "Of course, we can't handle Corbin alone! He's got this whole range in his pocket. He's run off one good man after another. He's about to take Polly Benson's spread. That's Duke's mother. And he's about to take Dan Benson's spread, too. Dan knows it, but he's so jealous of Slug Fenner that he doesn't want to admit it to you. I hate Fenner. I loathe him. Corbin made Slug town marshal because he could use him. I knew that, and I tried to play along, because I knew how helpless we were and I had hoped… Her voice died down.

Then she resumed almost defiantly, "Well, you're Silver Trent. Will you help us?"

At Silver's side, Magpie grunted sardonically and Jim Clane said in a high mincing voice, "Oh, please help us Mr. Robin Hood!"

Lars Johanssen roared. "Har! Har! T'ank you, Mister Robin. We don't want nothin' but to—"

Trent's furious voice cut across the roar like a whirlwind slicing through a boisterous breeze. "Shut up!"

The sudden violence of his anger set Magpie's jaw to dropping and had Lars looking at him with his china-blue eyes bulging.

Silver addressed the girl with strained politeness, "I am here only for my own profit. That must be clearly understood. I hear that Corbin has rustled a lot of cattle. I am an outlaw, and I can't afford to dole out charity. It happens, unfortunately, that I have surrounded myself with fools and half-wits. That is my hard luck, and I will not bore you with it. I intend to have cattle. It is up to you and your father whether I end by helping you as well as myself."

He swung suddenly on the older man. "What do you say, Kilvane. Do you want to play?"

The oldster granted. "I'm not in shape to say no, Trent."

"Then how many men have you got to help out?"

"Two hands at the place. They wasn't hired for fightin' men, but I figure they'll stick."

"That's three, including you," Silver said rapidly. "I've got a few more that I can leave you." He swung, blazing eyed on his gang. "Ricardo, Gomez, Stillson, Pablo—" he snapped. "You'll go with Mr. Kilvane—Pablo's in charge, of course. Don't try anything on your own, Pablo. Just keep them busy if they try to raid the ranch. I'll take the smart hombres with me. The ones that think they're fit to run things." He glared savagely at Magpie and Jim Clane and Lars. "Maybe I'll be able to make out with them, and maybe I won't!"

He spun his horse and rode back down the trail. Slowly, a little sullenly, Jim Clane, Magpie and Lars followed him on their horses.

He was half a hundred paces down before the voice came to him. Silver recognized it as the hard voice of Dan Benson: "Okay, Trent. I'll play your way, so there's eight of us instead of seven. But you're a damn fool. Corbin's got the men and he's smart. You'll run yourself into a noose."

Silver called back, *"Bueno, amigo,"* and went on, grinning a little in spite of the anger that still ran in him....

THEY HAD picked up the cattle, and now the lead steers ran into the carcass of a dead donkey and boggled at it, their heads down, swaying excitedly. Then they turned in panic and tried to swing off into the arroyo at the left. Silver cursed wearily and jumped the gaunted palomino to cut them off.

The steers swung back too far and tried to run down the grassy wash that twisted back toward the hills. Behind them, the herd began to pile up, bellowing and indecisive, turning first to one side and then another.

Silver sent the palomino to the other side and headed them off.

But the jam got worse.

155

Magpie Myers burst out of the canyon, crowding the steers, his horse knocked momentarily off balance and lunging against the canyon side so that Magpie's leg was crushed and scraped.

His blue, exhausted eyes took in the situation at a glance. "Take it easy or they will stampede," he called.

He eased his horse forward, shed his shirt and freed his rope. He made a short loop and tossed it deftly over the lead steer's horns and then he flipped his shirt over the steer's head and eyes, flipping over another loop to hold the cloth firm.

The blinded steer stopped short, bellowed, shook his head and looked about to stampede. Magpie put pressure on the rope, leading him carefully to windward of the dead donkey.

The others followed, snorting, snuffy, but quiet enough.

Far behind, the voice of Lars Johannssen sounded, "Gat alo-ong leetle doogies…."

It sounded fresh and careless and to Trent, who had not slept for three nights, a little irritating.

He said to Magpie, "Nice trick. We'd have had trouble there if it wasn't for you. I sure got plenty to learn about cows."

Magpie grunted and turned back to take his place.

Silver shrugged and let him go. Nobody but Lars had spoken to him unnecessarily after that night on the road when he had lost his temper. Lars had said, shamefacedly, "Hall! Silver. No use gatting soore."

But Magpie and Jim were thoroughly unforgiving.

Silver shook his head. He had looked full at Magpie's face before the oldster turned away, and Magpie was a lot more tired than Silver was. His face looked drawn and exhausted, with the deep lined wrinkles of old age drawn into the hard furrows of exhaustion. But his eyes had been alive and bright with hostility.

That deeply smouldering mutinous attitude was something that Silver could not disregard. He had to deal with it. But at the moment he didn't know how.

He led the herd down to the grassy depression which he had noted beforehand and turned, hard-eyed, toward his men. "Hold them here," he said curtly, and rode off.

The herd was here on Corbin's land. Would Corbin find them before the job was completed? He wondered if he had been underestimating Corbin. Fenner must have told him the whole thing by now. No, on second thought, Fenner wouldn't dare. But Corbin was shrewd enough to have guessed.

He shrugged the questions aside. At any event, the answer would appear shortly.

He turned his horse toward the K&K, putting him at a fast run and following the wooded ridge above the Corbin spread.

It was middle afternoon, with the sun hammering hot when he hit the K&K. Half a mile away he pulled up short and cursed.

Before him, were the smouldering ruins of what had evidently been a ranch house.

The stone chimney still stood and a part of one blackened wall. Behind it, the corral made a black, burned ring like a circle drawn in crayon by a child. To one side the barn was an irregular heap of charred ruins.

Silver drew a long breath, trying to lift the sudden, leaden weight of his heart. This was one time he had badly miscalculated this. He wouldn't have thought that Corbin would have the force, the power…. Not with men like Pablo and the others.

A rustle in the brush sent his hand down and up, gun freighted.

"Aqui estoy yo, Jefe," a voice said quietly.

It was Pablo.

Silver looked at him.

"Yes, I know," Pablo said a little wearily, in Spanish. "But there were too many. We lost one man and they three, but still it was too many. It was best to draw away through use arroyo. I am sorry, Jefe, about the ranch house."

Silver said, "One of ours lost?"

Pablo shook his head. "One of the ranch hands," he said grimly.

Silver's jaw muscles tightened. It was an old story—that he should come into a situation and cost some man his life without willing it.

His square-cut homely face turned toward Pablo, questioning. "How many's Corbin got?"

"Maybe thirty, maybe forty," Pablo answered impassively. He looked at Silver as though he were reading the thoughts that whirled through his head. "And a muchacho—a kid they call Duke—told us he's seat for the law-die Rangers."

Silver nodded. "Yeah…. Duke. Hell of a name for a kid, ain't it?"

"What do you say, *Jefe?* And why?"

"Skip it," Silver said.

"Duke," Pablo said slowly. "I do not know thees word."

"It means a hombre that has obligations and damn seldom lives up to 'em," Silver said.

Pablo's face cleared. *"Duque,"* he said. "Yes. The grandees that are not. *Comprendo!"*

"To hell with that," Silver said. "Would you like to ride with me? It looks like some of our crowd wouldn't."

FOOTSTEPS SOUNDED, coming through the brush. Silver stiffened a little but Pablo paid no attention.

He looked at Silver. "I have not told you everything," he said, his lean face impassive. "In retreating, it was necessary to leave certain ones behind. The *haciendero* of this—er—*hacienda.* In running, his daughter's horse was shot and she was thrown heavily. He was bullheaded to go after her, but that is what this gringo madman did. He was shot. We could do nothing. Both fell prisoners."

He stopped and his face lost color at the look of Silver's eyes.

After a moment he said: "Silver, I think you are confused because the others wish you to make profit out of your foolishness. For me, *no me gusta*—I do not care for it… But this is nothing—*denada.* Are you a child to quarrel with angry children? Or to look at me so? I am not a coward—this, I think, you have seen."

Silver looked at him. "So? But those I entrusted to you are gone."

Pablo caught his breath.

"I heard that!" a voice said bruskly. "I know enough Mex to get that, all right An', by God, you've said it! They run out on us, damn it!"

It was Dan Benson, his face suffused with rage, and his left arm in a sling.

Silver's eyes tuned on him coldly. "In that case, just now are you here?"

Pablo laughed softly. "He tried, this caballero, but a hit in the shoulder shocks a man. We were able to get him back, but not his companions."

Silver's voice dropped several degrees in temperature. "It looks like you've been lucky, young man," he said. "In your place I wouldn't complain of it—or presume on it. You've been in better fightin' hands than you're likely to be in for a long while."

Pablo's face split into a grin. "You have run into a family quarrel, young man. You are an outsider, so you are the one that gets the brickbats. Let this be a lesson to you."

Silver shook his shoulders impatiently. "Get the others. We're riding."

Pablo put his fingers to his lips and whistled. They rode up fast, leading Pablo's horse.

Silver saw that Gomez had a bandage around his chest. The rest were unmarked. He led them at a steady trot back to the herd.

Pablo laughed shortly at the sight of them. He bent forward, reading brands. Then he greeted Magpie with a grin.

"Well, old one," he jibed, "are you satisfied? It is plain to the eye that you have found all the stolen cattle. Now we will profit, eh?"

"I'll have to see the profit first before I count it," Magpie said bitterly. "I don't see us movin' to the Border with 'em."

Silver laughed at him. "Why, Magpie, these are cows that belong to the ranchers around here. Drive 'em down. We're delivering them."

Magpie glared and Jim Lane cursed.

It was sunset when they hit the flats, and full dusk before Silver, with Dan Benson's help, led the herd to within full sight of Corbin's ranch house.

Silver could just make out a corral full of horses, and figures that seemed to swarm out into the yard as though they had seen him and the herd.

Silver laughed. "Drive 'em to the house," he yelled. "We want to deliver them in style. Make 'em run!"

He whipped the gaunted palomino about and raced him toward the tail of the herd. "Come on, Lars, Jim, Magpie—run 'em straight for the ranch house!" His guns blasted and the herd jumped into life.

Jim Clane howled and his sixgun crashed.

The herd began to mill, changed its mind, burst into a sudden hammering, terrifying run, all in one direction.

Silver hollered exultantly, racing out after them, keeping the flank so that they should not turn.

He had been a cowhand enough to know the bitter disaster of a stampeding herd and the long work afterward, gathering them together—in case you out-lived the tossing, clicking horns and the mad hoofs thundering so blindly. Remembering that, it was strange to *make* a stampede.

And this herd was bellied out now to run straight and blind toward J.G. Corbin's ranch house.

Silver ran the palomino with them, stretched out, keeping the flank of the leading steers running straight....

CHAPTER 4
"HELL'S HAWKS FOR TRENT!"

THE DUSK was deeper now. He saw lights flash on in the ranch house, and knew, somehow, that men were yelling to each other there. He grinned, with the thunder of the herd in his ears. He was returning this range's stolen cattle, returning them all intact and in a way J.G. Corbin could hardly have expected.

And he wondered whether even this onslaught would overcome odds of five to one....

Then he forgot all that because the herd was trying to split, swerving outward on each side to miss the bulk of the first outbuilding in front of the main house. And now, above the hammering thunder of the hoofs he heard the crack of guns.

One of the lead steers went down, whipping its body over a broken neck. And steers piled up, bellowing madly, then the ones behind broke over and swerved.

Silver raced toward the head, his six-gun hammering and his voice high-pitched.

But they split at the outbuilding, all right, helped by the hammer of gunfire from the ranch yard, and then swept in a great dividing wave around the place.

Silver pulled up, waited for them to pass and then as the drag steers hammered past in the darkness, he lifted his famous full-throated battle-cry: "To me, *Los Halcones!* Hell's Hawks for Trent."

Even to his own ears the wild familiar call had a sudden overwhelming thrill, as though, listening to it, men's hearts might chill and stop—or start and warm as they never had before.

It lifted high and savage from his own bursting throat and echoed fiercely from the throats of his men. And he thought, if we never ride again, this is good!

He thought that, hammering straight toward the ranch house, knowing that his men were behind him, that they had understood his strategy even before he had started it.

His throat burst again in the old wild yell and crimson gun-flame blossomed from the yard, the bunkhouse and the ranch house. His guns jumped into his hands and responded, seeking out the spurting fire, hammering against his palms in the old remembered way.

And then the ranch house flashed by him, with a gun biting at him viciously as he passed. He pulled the palomino up to a rearing, wild-headed halt and slid from the saddle tutting the ground hard.

His hand swept to his saddle bags and came out with a bottle which he broke sharply against the back porch.

Beyond him, around him, behind him, shots hammered out, and Ricardo's horse pounded by half out of control, with Ricardo's guns slapping the night.

Silver's thumb nail struck a match, tossed it down where the bottle had broken, and the fumes of kerosene lifted.

The flared match made a yellow circle of light around him and the up-flicking blue of the kerosene flames took up from there.

Lead smacked Silver hard in the ribs and sent him whirling to the ground. He lay there an instant with the slugs whipping around him into the dirt, wondering briefly whether it was J.G. Corbin who had gotten that shot in. Yet he knew that it wasn't, because somehow he was certain that Corbin was in the house. Corbin, Kilvane—and Anne Kilvane.

He had needed only sight of Corbin to tell him what he was up against, and what this range was up against; needed only the realization that a gun-trap had been set for him which would have been deadly had he not prepared for it.

Slug Fenner didn't really matter in this because Slug was a yellow weakling, only an agent to get things started. The real man was Corbin....

It seemed to him, vaguely, that the light was getting brighter. He supposed that it must be because the flames were flaring up along the dry wood of the porch. Faintly he heard Ricardo yelling to him.

And then Ricardo took a slug and went down, and the back door of the ranch house opened. A round, sausage-made figure stood there in the crackling flare of the porch fire and grinned down at him. Deliberately then, Corbin lifted a sixgun and put its black muzzle on him.

"You shouldn't have got yourself shot, Trent," the big, rounded figure said to him, grinning wolfishly.

Against Trent's palm an unexpected, unthought of Colt

blasted. The sixgun in Corbin's hands jumped upward, exploded, whipped backward to slam against the boards of the porch.

Trent jumped to his feet, running to get out of the flare of light that targeted him, and pulling up his gun to fire again.

His foot caught on something and he fell flat and hard, the sixgun jumping out of his hand.

Corbin hurled himself forward, landed with his knees in Silver's back against his lungs, driving the breath out of him. He heaved, throwing the weight off.

Corbin fell sideways, caught himself on an elbow and whipped up with his fist slugging for Trent's ear as Trent got to his knees and slugged savagely. The blow slapped Corbin backward.

Silver saw that Corbin was getting to his feet. He struggled up also, thinking that this cylindrical man couldn't get to his feet any more than he, Silver, could.

Corbin stood swaying an instant and then hit Silver square on the mouth. Silver went back two paces and then stuck out his left and danced in, sinking his right into Corbin's stomach.

They came together then, and for the first time a full realization of what was happening came to Silver. He understood that so far sheer luck had helped him escape death at Corbin's hands. And he realized that he, Silver, had miscalculated because he had meant to arrange it so that Kilvane and his daughter could get out of the house safely before the thing burned down. But now he was in the grip of a man who was stronger than any other man he had come to grips with. A man who felt the urgent necessity of killing Silver here and now.

Corbin's big cylindrical arms began to squeeze, and Silver's cracked ribs were a sear of utter agony. He brought his knee up, shoving himself away. Corbin's grip broke and Silver hit him with everything he had and looked for him to go down. But he only staggered back and stooped to scoop up the dropped gun. And then it was that Silver knew he was caught....

IN FRONT and at the other side of the house the hammer of gunfire was still going on, and everything would be all right if he could keep from being killed.

Corbin jerked the gun up and pulled the trigger. Silver held his breath until he realized that the sharp click he heard was the snap of a hammer on an empty shell. In the same instant, he heard a terrified voice yelling, "Put 'em up, Corbin, or I'll drill you."

He stood up and slugged, the blow driving Corbin stumbling backward. And the same treble voice was yelling, "I tell ya, I'll shoot!"

Silver glimpsed a fantastically small figure with a squirrel rifle too big for him at his shoulder, and then something hit Corbin. The big body jerked, sagged and went down.

For a split second he wondered insanely if it could have been the kid. And then Slug Fenner's figure stepped out of the dark edging the firelight.

Fenner stood looking down at the man he had killed. He laughed and said, "He won't run no more ranges."

"Nor you no more double crosses," Magpie Myers said grimly, and shot him.

166

Silver turned toward the corner of the blazing house from which Magpie had emerged.

"Sometimes, old timer," he said, "you surprise even me."

A small, taut, hysterical figure appeared in front of him. "I'd of shot him, Silver," Duke cried. "I'd have shot him shore, if that other hombre hadn't of."

Silver looked at him and the squirrel rifle which had a ramrod still plugged into the muzzle, but be couldn't smile. Instead he said gently and soberly. "You're a good man, son."

The kid burst suddenly into wild tears, and Silver picked him up and held him close. "Take it easy, old timer," he said.

He became aware all at once that people were around him and that the gunfire had stopped. Jim Clane was there and Pablo and Magpie and Lars and Kilvane and his girl and that hot-headed youngster, Benson, who had his arm around Anne Kilvane.

Silver grinned. He said: "Looks like I've hardly got to know you folks, yet what we was supposed to do was to kind of help you out."

Old man Kilvane stared at him and then laughed unbelievingly. "*Kind* of help us out! Hell, if anybody ever gets helped out better, anywhere, I sure hope to be around to see it. This range is plumb clean!"

Anne Kilvane looked at Silver. "It's not only clean. We—we saw the cows you drove in here I'm guessin' that they're most of those that have been rustled."

Silver looked at her. "Why, yes, ma'am. I reckon they are. An' returned with the compliments of *Los Halcones*." He bowed and looked at Jim Clane and Magpie Myers. "Though," he went on, "some of my men kind of think we ought to have taken them for our own profit."

Jim Clane's face grew red in the light of Corbin's blazing house. "You—you're damn right," he choked. "You—"

Silver ignored him. "Instead," he said tranquilly to the girl, "we figure to take Corbin's cattle. That will pay us out pretty good."

Magpie Myers looked at him and suddenly burst out laughing.

Lars Johannseen bellowed, "Jeeminy, he's right I see them cows. This Corbin, he has yust made his round-up. He is waiting to get through his lighting before he drives to market Hall! D'ere ain't more than two fallows wit' d'at herd."

Jim Clane looked at Silver and shook his head. "All right," he said, "All right…." Silver grinned at him.

"There are more of them than there were in the rustled herd, Jim," he said, "but you don't care about that. All you really care about is gettin' argumentative."

Jim Clane grinned reluctantly. "What I cared about," he said, "was gettin' rid of that Fenner."

Ricardo, standing to one side, flashed his teeth. "For me," he said. "Yes. But that wasn't so much. But then, Jim, you forget. Silver wasn't fooled. No, I think not from the first minute."

Jim looked suddenly shame-faced. "Sure," he said. "Sure."

Silver suddenly put Duke Benson down to the ground. "Stand on your own feet," he hollered at him. "Ain't you a man?"

Duke looked startled. "Why—why, I guess not yet." Then

he grinned suddenly. "You ain't scarin' me, Silver.... Much," he added, pulling in his breath.

"You wait," Silver growled at him. "Your maw and your spread are safe now, an' in less than a week it'll have a palomino pony on it. You wait He'll be steppin' dainty wherever an' whenever you want him to go."

The kid breathed deep and his eyes were round. "Gee," he said softly, "That's swell. Havin' that, an' me havin' heard it. Gee, I reckon nothin' that big'll ever happen to me again."

Silver looked at him, puzzled. "Heard what."

Duke looked at him almost scornfully. "Why the yell," he said, as though he couldn't believe anybody was that dumb "Ev'ybody talks about it, but there ain't many, I bet that's really heard it. But I heard it!" He put back his head suddenly with his eyes shining, in another world. "To me, *Los Halcones!*" he roared, deep-voiced. "Hell's Hawks for Trent!"

POPULAR HERO PULPS AVAILABLE NOW:

THE SPIDER

❏ #1: The Spider Strikes	$13.95
❏ #2: The Wheel of Death	$13.95
❏ #3: Wings of the Black Death	$13.95
❏ #4: City of Flaming Shadows	$13.95
❏ #5: Empire of Doom!	$13.95
❏ #6: Citadel of Hell	$13.95
❏ #7: The Serpent of Destruction	$13.95
❏ #8: The Mad Horde	$13.95
❏ #9: Satan's Death Blast	$13.95
❏ #10: The Corpse Cargo	$13.95
❏ #11: Prince of the Red Looters	$13.95
❏ #12: Reign of the Silver Terror	$13.95
❏ #13: Builders of the Dark Empire	$13.95
❏ #14: Death's Crimson Juggernaut	$13.95
❏ #15: The Red Death Rain	$13.95
❏ #16: The City Destroyer	$13.95
❏ #17: The Pain Emperor	$13.95
❏ #18: The Flame Master	$13.95
❏ #19: Slaves of the Crime Master	$13.95
❏ #20: Reign of the Death Fiddler	$13.95
❏ #21: Hordes of the Red Butcher	$13.95
❏ #22: Dragon Lord of the Underworld	$13.95
❏ #23: Master of the Death-Madness	$13.95
❏ #24: King of the Red Killers	$13.95
❏ #25: Overlord of the Damned	$13.95
❏ #26: Death Reign of the Vampire King	$13.95
❏ #27: Emperor of the Yellow Death	$13.95
❏ #28: The Mayor of Hell	$13.95
❏ #29: Slaves of the Murder Syndicate	$13.95
❏ #30: Green Globes of Death	$13.95
❏ #31: The Cholera King	$13.95
❏ #32: Slaves of the Dragon	$13.95
❏ #33: Legions of Madness	$12.95
❏ #34: Laboratory of the Damned	$12.95
❏ #35: Satan's Sightless Legion	$12.95
❏ #36: The Coming of the Terror	$12.95
❏ #37: The Devil's Death-Dwarfs	$12.95
❏ #38: City of Dreadful Night	$12.95
❏ #39: Reign of the Snake Men	$12.95

❏ #40: Dictator of the Damned	$12.95
❏ #41: The Mill-Town Massacres	$12.95
❏ #42: Satan's Workshop	$12.95
❏ #43: Scourge of the Yellow Fangs	$12.95
❏ #44: The Devil's Pawnbroker	$12.95
❏ 45: Voyage of the Coffin Ship	$12.95
❏ #46: The Man Who Ruled in Hell	$13.95
❏ #47: Slaves of the Black Monarch	$13.95
❏ #48: Machineguns Over the White House	$13.95
❏ *NEW*: #49: The City That Dared Not Eat	$13.95

THE WESTERN RAIDER

❏ #1: Guns of the Damned	$13.95
❏ #2: The Hawk Rides Back from Death	$13.95
❏ #3: Gun-Call for the Lost Legion	$13.95
❏ #4: The Law of Silver Trent	$13.95
❏ #5: The Gun-Prayer of Silver Trent	$13.95
❏ *NEW*: #6: Silver Trent Rides Alone	$13.95

G-8 AND HIS BATTLE ACES

❏ #1: The Bat Staffel	$13.95

CAPTAIN SATAN

❏ #1: The Mask of the Damned	$13.95
❏ #2: Parole for the Dead	$13.95
❏ #3: The Dead Man Express	$13.95
❏ #4: A Ghost Rides the Dawn	$13.95
❏ #5: The Ambassador From Hell	$13.95

DR. YEN SIN

❏ #1: Mystery of the Dragon's Shadow	$12.95
❏ #2: Mystery of the Golden Skull	$12.95
❏ #3: Mystery of the Singing Mummies	$12.95

CAPTAIN ZERO

❏ #1: City of Deadly Sleep	$13.95
❏ #2: The Mark of Zero!	$13.95
❏ #3: The Golden Murder Syndicate	$13.95

POPULAR HERO PULPS ℗ AVAILABLE NOW:

THE SECRET 6
❏ #1: The Red Shadow $13.95
❏ #2: House of Walking Corpses $13.95
❏ #3: The Monster Murders $13.95
❏ #4: The Golden Alligator $13.95

OPERATOR 5
❏ #1: The Masked Invasion $13.95
❏ #2: The Invisible Empire $13.95
❏ #3: The Yellow Scourge $13.95
❏ #4: The Melting Death $13.95
❏ #5: Cavern of the Damned $13.95
❏ #6: Master of Broken Men $13.95
❏ #7: Invasion of the Dark Legions $13.95
❏ #8: The Green Death Mists $13.95
❏ #9: Legions of Starvation $13.95
❏ #10: The Red Invader $13.95
❏ #11: The League of War-Monsters $13.95
❏ #12: The Army of the Dead $13.95
❏ #13: March of the Flame Marauders $13.95
❏ #14: Blood Reign of the Dictator $13.95
❏ #15: Invasion of the Yellow Warlords $13.95
❏ #16: Legions of the Death Master $13.95
❏ #17: Hosts of the Flaming Death $13.95
❏ #18: Invasion of the Crimson Death Cult $13.95
❏ #19: Attack of the Blizzard Men $13.95
❏ #20: Scourge of the Invisible Death $13.95
❏ #21: Raiders of the Red Death $13.95
❏ #22: War-Dogs of the Green Destroyer $13.95
❏ #23: Rockets From Hell $13.95
❏ #24: War-Masters from the Orient $13.95
❏ #25: Crime's Reign of Terror $13.95
❏ #26: Death's Ragged Army $13.95
❏ #27: Patriots' Death Battalion $13.95

DUSTY AYRES AND HIS BATTLE BIRDS
❏ #1: Black Lightning! $13.95
❏ #2: Crimson Doom $13.95
❏ #3: The Purple Tornado $13.95
❏ #4: The Screaming Eye $13.95
❏ #5: The Green Thunderbolt $13.95
❏ #6: The Red Destroyer $13.95
❏ #7: The White Death $13.95
❏ #8: The Black Avenger $13.95
❏ #9: The Silver Typhoon $13.95
❏ #10: The Troposphere F-S $13.95
❏ #11: The Blue Cyclone $13.95
❏ #12: The Tesla Raiders $13.95

MAVERICKS
❏ #1: Five Against the Law $12.95
❏ #2: Mesquite Manhunters $12.95
❏ #3: Bait for the Lobo Pack $12.95
❏ #4: Doc Grimson's Outlaw Posse $12.95
❏ #5: Charlie Parr's Gunsmoke Cure $12.95

THE MYSTERIOUS WU FANG
❏ #1: The Case of the Six Coffins $12.95
❏ #2: The Case of the Scarlet Feather $12.95
❏ #3: The Case of the Yellow Mask $12.95
❏ #4: The Case of the Suicide Tomb $12.95
❏ #5: The Case of the Green Death $12.95
❏ #6: The Case of the Black Lotus $12.95
❏ #7: The Case of the Hidden Scourge $12.95